147th Street
Herman's Apartment
145th Street
P.S. 737
144th Street
Central Harlem Animal Hospital
Mr. Jones's Apartment
143rd Street
142nd Street
Post Office
Harlem Hospital
FIFTH AVE.
MADISON AVE.
HARLEM RIVER DRIVE
HARLEM RIVER
Bridge
Madison Avenue Bridge
Third Avenue Bridge
MAJOR DEEGAN EXPRESSWAY
Mr. Ritchie's
La Finca del Sur Community Garden
SOUTH BRONX
N
W
E
S

THE VANDERBEEKERS

to the RESCUE

THE VANDERBEEKERS to the RESCUE

By Karina Yan Glaser

HOUGHTON MIFFLIN HARCOURT
BOSTON NEW YORK

hmhbooks.com

The text was set in Stempel Garamond.

Library of Congress Cataloging-in-Publication Data
Names: Glaser, Karina Yan, author.
Title: Vanderbeekers to the rescue / by Karina Yan Glaser.
Description: Boston ; New York : Houghton Mifflin Harcourt, [2019] | Series: The Vanderbeekers ; [3] | Summary: The Vanderbeeker children, ages six to thirteen, race to help save their mother's baking business from closure after it fails an inspection.
Identifiers: LCCN 2019001115 (print) | LCCN 2019002594 (ebook) | ISBN 9780358162117 (ebook) | ISBN 9781328577573 (hardback)
Subjects: | CYAC: Family life—New York (State)—Harlem—Fiction. | Bakers and bakeries—Fiction. | Pets—Fiction. | African Americans—Fiction. | Harlem (New York, N.Y.)—Fiction. | New York (N.Y.)—Fiction. | BISAC: JUVENILE FICTION / Family / Siblings. | JUVENILE FICTION / Lifestyles / City & Town Life. | JUVENILE FICTION / Social Issues / Friendship. | JUVENILE FICTION / Business, Careers, Occupations.
Classification: LCC PZ7.1.G5847 (ebook) | LCC PZ7.1.G5847 Vat 2019 (print) |DDC [Fic]—dc23
LC record available at https://lccn.loc.gov/2019001115

Printed in the United States of America
DOC 10 9 8 7 6 5 4 3 2 1
4500769325

To Katie, Lauren, and Harrigan,
fellow animal lovers
and sisters of my heart

"They keep coming up new all the time—
things to perplex you, you know. You settle
one question and there's another right after . . .
It keeps me busy all the time thinking them
over and deciding what's right."

—L. M. Montgomery, *Anne of Green Gables*

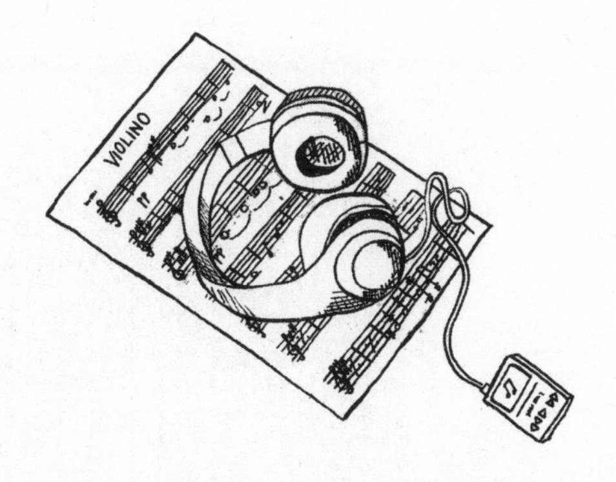

Sunday, February 24

One

It was a blustery, wintry afternoon on 141st Street. A blizzard was ripping up the East Coast, and the center of the storm had decided to stay on top of Harlem and hang out for a while. Meanwhile, the brownstones along the street stood strong and steady, protecting their inhabitants the same way they had for over a hundred years. While plows rumbled up and down the avenues, snow inched up the windowsills and dusted the bricks, engulfing parked cars and piling up on sidewalks.

In the exact middle of 141st Street sat a humble red brownstone with a weathervane currently covered in snow. The Vanderbeeker family lived on the ground and first floors of this brownstone, and at the moment they were all in the living room. Thirteen-year-old twins Jessie and Isa, ten-year-old Oliver, and eight-year-old Hyacinth were regretting that they had let Laney, newly turned six, choose the board game. She had selected the very one that could go on for hours. As they waited their turn to roll the dice, each yearned for warmer weather, spring bulbs peeking up through the earth, and getting dirty in the community garden they had created for their upstairs neighbors the year before.

When her phone rang, Mama weaved through kids, pets, and stacks of books to grab it from the side table by the door. The Vanderbeekers heard her say "Really?" and "Of course!" and "That would be wonderful!" As her voice grew in volume and enthusiasm, the Vanderbeeker kids paused from their game.

Papa, who was wearing his favorite pair of forest-green coveralls and attempting to fix a leak in the kitchen sink, put down his wrench and made his way toward Mama to see what was going on. When she hung up, her whole family was surrounding her. Her eyes were bright with a mixture of excitement and astonishment.

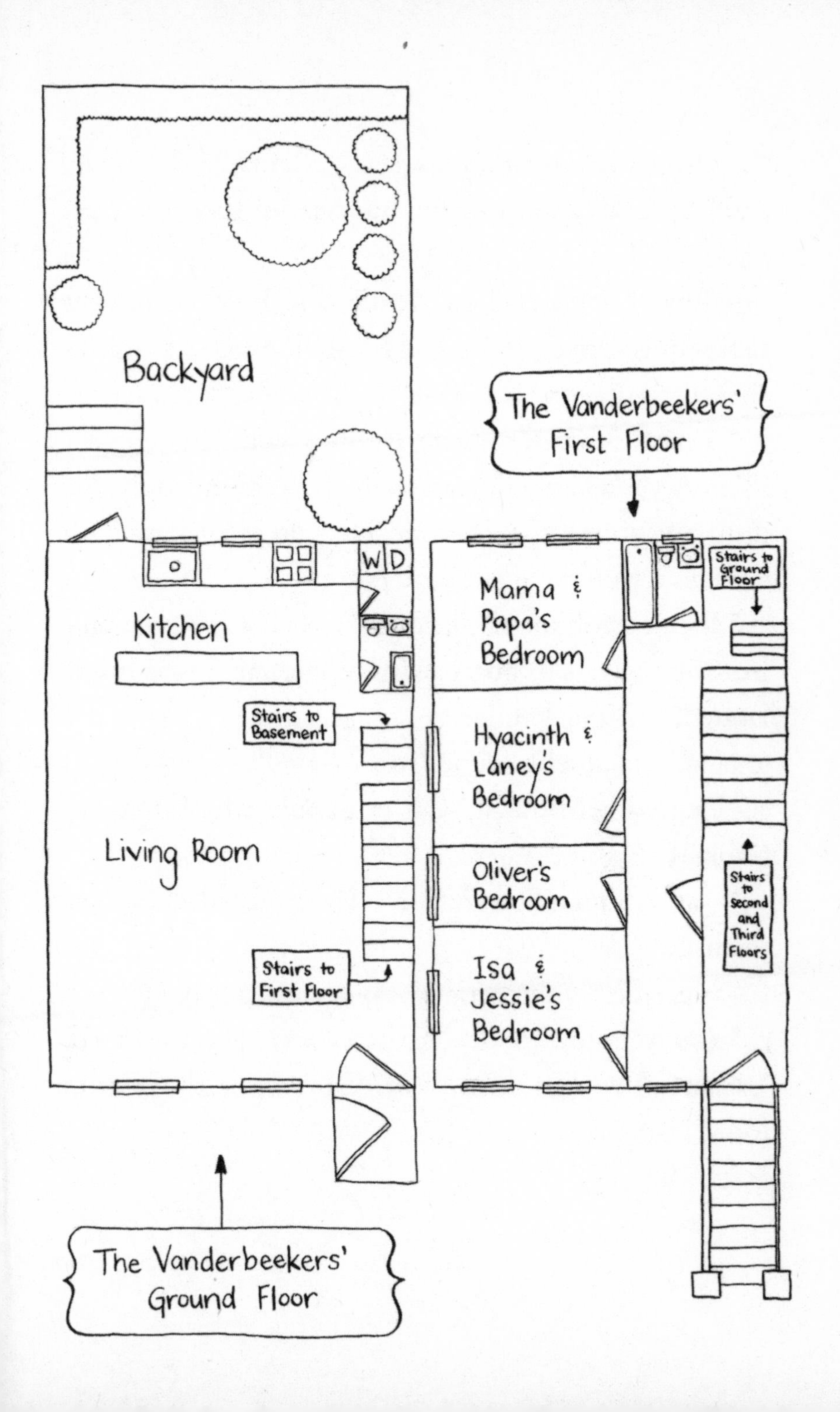
Backyard
The Vanderbeekers' First Floor
W
D
Kitchen
Mama & Papa's Bedroom
Stairs to Ground Floor
Hyacinth & Laney's Bedroom
Stairs to Basement
Living Room
Oliver's Bedroom
Stairs to second and Third Floors
Stairs to First Floor
Isa & Jessie's Bedroom
The Vanderbeekers' Ground Floor

"That was *Perch Magazine,*" Mama said. "They want to feature me and my business in their October issue."

"What?" screeched Isa, Jessie, and Hyacinth at the same time. Oliver, Papa, and Laney looked at one another in confusion.

"What's *Birch Magazine*?" Oliver said.

"*Perch Magazine,*" Isa clarified. "And it's only the most amazing magazine ever. They do interviews with awesome women, like Hope Jahren—"

"She's a geobiologist known for her work on stable isotope analysis to analyze fossil forests!" Jessie interrupted.

"—and Jacqueline Woodson—"

"I know her books!" Oliver exclaimed. "I *love* her books!"

"—and Sonia Sotomayor," Isa finished, her face flushed.

"Supreme Court justice!" Hyacinth squeaked.

"You're going to be on the cover?" Laney asked. "What are you going to wear? Can I be in the picture too?"

Mama looked dazed. "I'm definitely *not* going to be on the cover. They have a section about small-business owners, and they want to feature me. I have no idea how they even know me! Someone from the magazine must have gone to an event where my desserts were served. There will be a whole magazine spread about my cookies! They're going to send a photographer to the brownstone!"

Papa pulled Mama into a hug and started doing a little dance with her at the bottom of the stairs. "I'm so proud of you."

Jessie took out her phone, opened the web browser, and typed madly with her thumbs. "Holy smokes, listen to these circulation numbers. Eight hundred thousand print copies and over two million unique views on their website every month!"

"You're going to be famous!" Laney yelled, hopping around them.

"Now *everyone* is going to want your cookies," Oliver said, mentally calculating how Mama's increased business might positively affect his weekly allowance.

"You're going to need a website and a wholesale list," Isa said wisely.

"How do you know that?" Jessie asked.

"Benny has to do it for Castleman's Bakery," Isa said.

"When is the photo shoot?" Papa asked.

"The first week in April," Mama said.

"That's when your birthday is!" Laney yelled. "On April sixth!"

Mama's hands flew to her cheeks as she looked around the brownstone. The Vanderbeekers followed her gaze, and suddenly they saw their home as a fancy magazine photographer might. Franz, their basset hound, was methodically removing toys from his basket and strategically placing them in areas with the most foot traffic. Hay was strewn on the floor from Paganini, Laney's rabbit, who kicked as much of it as possible when jumping out of his box. George Washington, their orange-and-white tabby, was batting at the loose threads from the fabric of their couch, which was fraying because he used the furniture to sharpen his claws (even though there were two scratching posts in the living room).

And then there were the piles of books, the odds and ends of Jessie's science experiments, and Isa's sheet music tossed on various surfaces. Oliver's basketball was wedged under an armchair, and Hyacinth's treasure box gaped open, yarn in a dozen colors spilling out in every direction.

Jessie spoke first. "We can totally make this brownstone magazine-worthy."

Oliver was skeptical. "We can?"

Isa stood up straighter. "Of course we can!"

Papa touched the living room walls. "I've been meaning to patch and paint the walls. And refinish the floors. And build some more bookcases, because obviously five huge bookcases aren't enough for us. I can do that by April."

Mama's jaw began to relax.

"Mama, trust us," Isa told her. "We've got this."

The family gathered around her and did a communal Vanderbeeker fist bump.

"Fame and fortune, here we come!" Oliver yelled.

APRIL

MONDAY	TUESDAY	WEDNESDA
1	2	3

← S·P·R·I·N·G

Monday, April 1

One month, eight days later

THURSDAY	FRIDAY	SATURDAY
4	5 Perch Magazine Photo Shoot! Isa's Audition	6 Mama's Birthday!
B·R·E·A·K	→	→

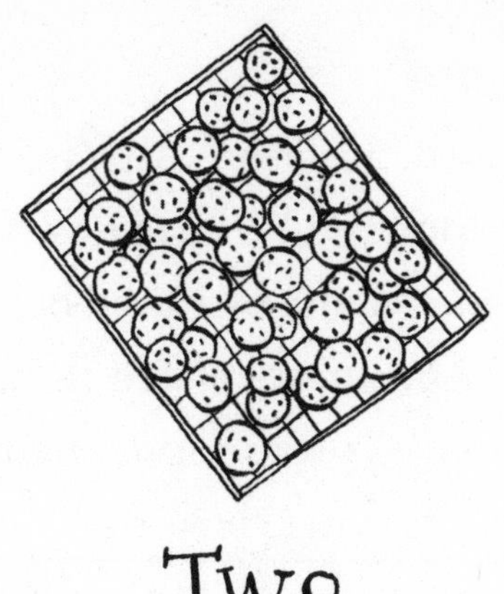

Two

It turned out that thirty-six days were not nearly enough to make the apartment magazine-ready. The past month had been full of unexpected emergencies. Laney had had her tonsils removed and lived on milk-shakes and applesauce for days. Oliver had sprained two fingers while playing basketball and wore splints for three weeks, and when his fingers had healed, he'd then managed to run his bike into a tree and ended up in the emergency room for x-rays. (He was fine.) Hyacinth had come down with an ear infection, strep throat, and pinkeye at the same time. Isa and Jessie were dragging under the weight of increased home-work, and Isa had also been practicing violin in the basement every day for hours in preparation for an upcoming orchestra audition. Papa had been assigned a big project at work and had been working late nights and weekends, and Mama had been baking nonstop in addition to doing business-related things like creating a website, developing promotional items, and preparing for the magazine interview.

Now it was spring break, and it was a big week. There were only five days until the *Perch Magazine* photo shoot on Friday, which also happened to be the day of Isa's audition, and Mama's birthday was on Saturday. As a result, the apartment was even more chaotic than usual.

"We need a game plan," Isa told her siblings, who were scattered throughout the living room.

Laney was rearranging books to build a maze for Paganini. She believed mazes would make the rabbit even smarter than he already was. Hyacinth was kneeling on the floor, her eyes two inches from the carpet, trying to locate a sewing needle she had dropped. Over on the couch, Jessie was highlighting nearly every sentence in a science book she had found for fifty cents at the library sale. Oliver was staring out the window at the relentless rain and muttering to himself.

"Did you know that the idea of absolute motion or absolute rest is misleading?" Jessie said, not looking up from her book, her highlighter racing furiously over the pages. "This book is blowing my mind."

"I can't work on the treehouse with Uncle Arthur when it's raining like this," Oliver grumbled, pacing in front of the window before deciding that a snack would help him feel better. He made his way to the kitchen.

"Oliver, don't move!" Hyacinth exclaimed. She was still searching for her needle, which she had dropped while making a felt birthday hat for Mama. "I don't want you to step on the needle!"

Isa crossed her arms, annoyed at her siblings. "Did anyone hear what I just said?"

"Nope," Oliver said, frozen, scanning the carpet for a glint of silver. "Hey, does all this work we're doing to get the apartment ready count as Mama's birthday present?"

Isa glared at him. "She's turning forty. That's a big birthday."

Oliver shook his head. "Maybe we should think of doing one family birthday party once a year. There are too many people in this family to keep track of."

"I don't like that idea at all," said Laney, who loved birthdays more than any holiday or other celebration.

"Did you know—" Jessie began, looking up from her science book again.

"Listen up," Isa interrupted. "We promised Mama we would help her."

"I *have* helped," Laney said, looking at Isa. "I chose my outfit for the photo shoot, and I made some new pictures for the walls, and—"

Jessie finally put her book down. "You get to be in the photo shoot?"

"Yup," Laney said.

Jessie glanced at Isa, who gave a little shake of her head.

"We cleaned yesterday," Oliver said, referring to the ten-second vacuuming job he'd done in the living room. "The apartment looks great to me."

Isa pointed to the chalkboard hanging by the front door, where they had made a list of things to do for the photo shoot. "We haven't done seventy-five percent of the things on that list."

Oliver looked at the chalkboard. "We *can't* do those things."

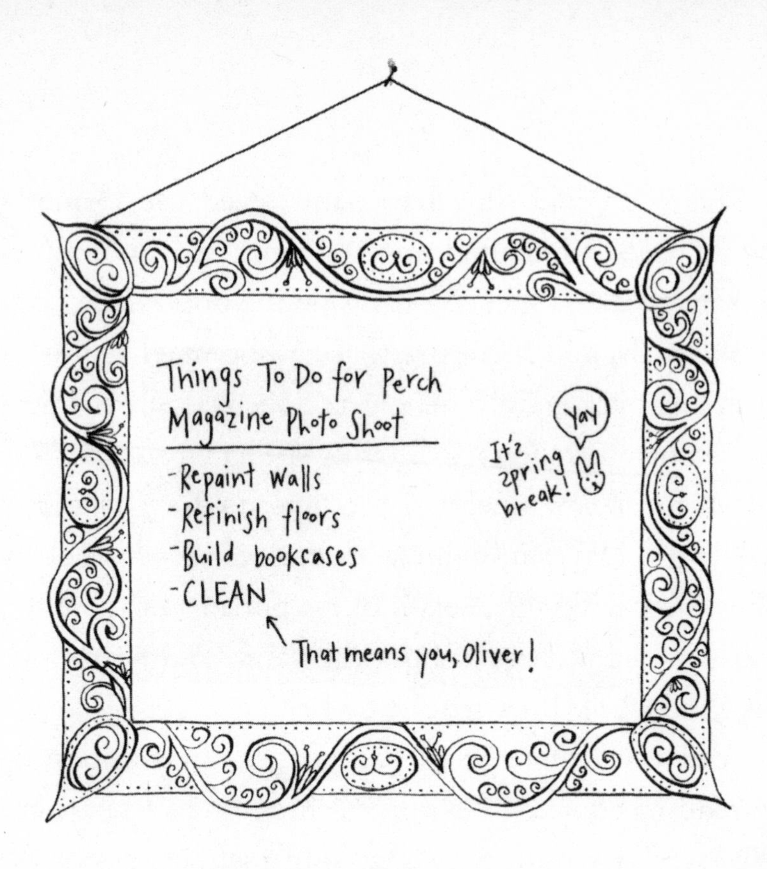

"Uncle Arthur is coming over," Isa said. "Maybe you guys can build the bookcases today."

Oliver made a face. "Uncle Arthur is supposed to be building *my* treehouse."

"It's raining," Jessie pointed out.

Oliver glared at the window, as if the weather were personally insulting him. "Fine. We'll do the bookcases."

"Now, what about these walls?" Isa said.

Hyacinth, who loved to paint, eyed the formerly white walls, which now sported years' worth of scuffs left by sneakers kicked off inside the doorway, errant basketballs, and furniture that had bumped against it over and over again. There were dozens of spots where Laney had torn down a drawing she had made to make room for a new one, and the tape holding it up had taken off a layer of paint with it. A darkened spot by the window was the result of Isa putting a candle too close to the wall, scorching the paint, and nearly setting the whole brownstone on fire.

And then there were the gouges. In addition to shredding couches, George Washington had a particular love for running his claws against corners of the walls, where thin, deep grooves rose two feet high.

"I asked Mama about painting the living room," Hyacinth said as she continued her search for the missing needle, "but she said the supplies would cost three hundred dollars."

"Three hundred dollars!" Laney exclaimed. "You could buy a whole castle for that!"

Outside, wind and rain lashed at the windows. The sky was dark with heavy clouds, making it seem like evening instead of noontime. Paganini huddled in his book maze, uncertain about his enclosure and the weather.

"Found it!" Hyacinth exclaimed, holding a sliver of silver in the air.

Oliver breathed a sigh of relief and continued to the kitchen. A crack of thunder sent George Washington bolting up the stairs to the second floor, where there were plenty of beds to hide under.

Oliver lingered by the kitchen, breathing in the smell of chocolate sea salt caramel cookies cooling on the counter. Mama had unwisely left the cookies unattended before she dashed out to a meeting with the editor at *Perch Magazine*. "I'll be back before the inspector comes," she had said before leaving.

"What inspector?" Isa had hollered back, but Mama had disappeared. Isa looked at Jessie, and Jessie shrugged.

"Probably a building inspector who wants to make sure the brownstone is up to code," Oliver had said knowledgeably. Uncle Arthur was a contractor, and Oliver loved nothing more than when his uncle came over and taught him how to handle power tools.

"Mama told me not to touch those cookies," Laney warned. "She told me three times."

"They're for a party," Isa said. "Library fundraiser or something."

"Mama won't miss *one* cookie," Oliver said, pulling the tray closer to the edge of the counter.

Hyacinth gave an objecting squeak, just as the doorbell rang.

Franz, who had been chasing a cat in his sleep, leaped to his feet and ran as fast as his short legs could take him to the front door. Oliver's curiosity about the doorbell ringer won out over the cookie stealing—for the moment—and he joined the scramble to see who it was.

First to get there after Franz was Laney. She slid the step stool in front of the door and stood on her tiptoes to glance through the peephole. "It's a stranger!" she reported.

"Back it up," Isa said while her younger siblings made way to let the twins through.

Jessie moved the step stool and looked through the peephole. A man about Papa's age was standing outside the door, juggling a clipboard and an umbrella, and the thing that stood out most to Jessie wasn't the rain pouring off his umbrella in a cascade of water or the large ID tag that said INSPECTOR in dark, bold letters. The thing that stood out most was his facial expression.

He did *not* look happy.

Three

Jessie opened the door but kept the security chain engaged so the door opened only a couple of inches. Her siblings crowded around to peer through the crack. "Can I help you?" Jessie asked.

"I'm Mr. West from New York State Department of Agriculture and Markets," the man said. "I'm a little early. I'm here to meet with"—he squinted at his clipboard—"a Mrs. Vanderbeeker."

"He must be the inspector Mama meant," Isa said to Jessie.

Franz gave another howl and jumped so one paw swiped through the sliver of open door. Mr. West sprang back and dropped his umbrella, which the wind stole and joyfully sent tumbling down the street before anyone could say "Mississippi."

"Crumb!" the man said. The Vanderbeekers watched him internally debate whether to chase the umbrella. Deciding it was pointless, he tucked his clipboard into his bag and pulled the hood of his jacket over his head.

"He said a bad word!" Laney said loudly.

"*Crumb* isn't a bad word," Jessie said.

"Yes, it is," Laney insisted.

"No, it isn't."

Jessie turned back to the door, where Mr. West was getting wetter by the second.

"Yes, it is," Laney whispered, just quietly enough for Jessie not to hear.

"Sorry about that," Isa said through the crack in the door. "Our dog gets overexcited. Mama should be back soon. Let me text her to see if I can let you in." Isa took out her phone and sent her mom a message. Then the five Vanderbeeker kids, plus Franz, who continued to howl and leap at the window, proceeded to watch the man get completely drenched.

"I'm sure she'll respond soon," Isa said apologetically. She dialed Mama's number, but it went straight to voice mail. "Do you want to come back later?"

Mr. West wiped raindrops from his eyes. "My department is severely understaffed. If we don't do it now, it will be months before I can get back here."

"Hold on one second, Mr. West." Jessie closed the door and turned to Isa. "Mama *did* say an inspector was coming. I'm sure it's fine to let him in."

"True," Isa said. "It might be worse if Mama misses this appointment. Remember the time Papa forgot about the boiler inspection? Boom, two-hundred-dollar fine."

Jessie thought about this, then removed the chain and opened the door. A very wet, very disgruntled-looking Mr. West stepped inside. Franz pushed his face into Mr. West's legs and started licking the bottom of his raincoat. Franz loved rainwater. When Mr. West realized what Franz was doing, he yanked his jacket away, and the kids recognized him immediately as Not a Dog Person. Hyacinth grabbed Franz's collar and tempted him into the living room with a shake of the dog-biscuit jar.

Meanwhile, Mr. West dripped a steady stream of water onto their area rug. A loud howl made everyone swivel to see George Washington flying down the stairs, his tummy swinging wildly from side to side. He skidded on the wooden floor when he reached the landing, then scrambled into the living room and hid behind a potted plant.

Mr. West pushed wet hair out of his eyes, pulled his clipboard from his bag, and wrote something down.

The Vanderbeekers soon saw the reason for George Washington's abrupt arrival and departure. Princess Cutie scrambled down the steps in a blur of white fur, then began meowing and pouncing around the living room in search of her archenemy. Despite many attempts to broker peace between the two cats, they remained quite antagonistic toward each other.

"You have *two* cats?" Mr. West asked.

"The orange one is ours," Laney said. "That white one belongs to Mr. Beiderman. Her name is Princess Cutie."

"She's staying with us until Mr. Beiderman gets back from his trip," Isa said, then turned to her siblings. "I cannot *wait* for her to leave. She talks *so* much!" Her siblings nodded in agreement.

"Mr. Beiderman is our landlord," Laney told Mr. West. "He also lives upstairs. He tried to evict us, but then he changed his mind."

"Jeez, Laney," Oliver said. "Oversharing."

"He didn't try to evict us," Jessie clarified. "He just wasn't going to renew our lease."

Mr. West wrote something else on his clipboard.

"What are you writing?" Laney inquired, standing on her tiptoes to peek at his paper.

Mr. West ignored her question and angled the clipboard away from her. "How many animals do you have in total?"

"Four," Laney said.

"But only three actually live here," Jessie said.

"We have a dog, a cat, and a rabbit," Laney said. "I want another rabbit, but Papa says no."

Mr. West checked something off on his clipboard. "Where's the rabbit?" he asked.

Laney pointed at the living room, and Mr. West peeked in. Paganini had managed to escape from his maze and was now sitting in the middle of the carpet, his narrowed eyes glinting at Mr. West with deep distrust. Mr. West cleared his throat and glanced around the rest of the apartment.

"Is there another kitchen here?" he asked.

"Why would we have another kitchen?" Jessie asked.

"Does anyone have more than one kitchen?" Oliver wondered out loud.

Before Mr. West could ask another question, Isa and Jessie both yelled, "Franz, no!"

Their shouts were followed by a crash, then a happy howl. Miraculously, Franz had managed to jump high enough on his short legs to bump his nose against the tray holding the precious batch of chocolate sea salt caramel cookies. The tray had been hanging slightly over the edge of the counter from when Oliver had considered stealing one. In a matter of seconds, all five Vanderbeeker kids plus Princess Cutie raced to the kitchen and skidded to a stop. Princess Cutie gleefully batted the cookies and sent them careening around the floor. One slid underneath the oven. Another went into the two-inch gap between the refrigerator and the cabinet. Hyacinth grabbed Franz's collar while Jessie tried to pry his mouth open and dig out the four cookies he had managed to snatch.

Laney kept yelling, "Chocolate is poisonous to animals!" over and over again until Isa intervened and gave her the job of holding Princess Cutie so she could gather the fallen cookies.

"Hyacinth, you owe me bigtime for saving your dog's life," Jessie said with a grimace, letting go of Franz and throwing away the mushed-up cookies she had scooped from his mouth.

"Maybe we should take him to the vet, just in case?" Hyacinth suggested, worried. "Chocolate poisoning in animals is very serious."

Mr. West cleared his throat, and the Vanderbeeker kids looked up in surprise. They had forgotten he was there!

Isa was the first to remember her manners. "Can I get you anything, Mr. West? A glass of water? A towel so you can dry off?"

Mr. West was still standing in a corner of the living room. Paganini was blocking his path to the rest of the apartment.

"How about a cookie?" Oliver called. "I saved about twenty of them! Five-second rule!"

"Many scientists dispute the five-second rule," Jessie said. "Most bacteria transfers to food immediately upon impact."

Mr. West shuddered and shook his head. "I do *not* want a cookie," he said to them before writing one final thing on his clipboard. Then he tore off a set of yellow carbon-copy sheets from under the paper he was writing on and said, "This visit was intended to be an inspection of the premises for your mother's home processor's license. There are serious violations."

"A *home processor's license?*" Oliver said. "I thought you were going to inspect the building or the boiler or something."

"This is for Mama's *baking* business?" Isa exclaimed.

Mr. West continued as if the Vanderbeekers had not said anything. "On behalf of the New York State Department of Agriculture and Markets, I am revoking the license until this kitchen can pass another inspection. An official letter will arrive shortly. Your mother must terminate all business operations until she meets the requirements and must request another inspection before she can resume her business." Mr. West slapped the yellow paper on an end table.

"You can't do that!" Jessie said. "She's going to be in *Perch Magazine*!"

"And she *needs* to work this week!" Isa called as Mr. West made his way to the door. He didn't respond. The door opened. Wind slipped inside the brownstone and gave a big roar. Then the door shut again, leaving only silence behind.

Four

Did what I think happened just happen?" Jessie asked her siblings when she found her voice.

"He was scared of Paganini," Laney reported. She skipped over to her rabbit and stroked his forehead. Paganini hunkered down, his eyes half closed in bliss. "Who could be scared of a sweet little rabbit?"

"This is not good," Jessie said, running her hands through her hair. "Jeez, Oliver, did you really have to offer him a cookie that had fallen on the floor?"

"I thought he was checking the boiler or the roof or something!" Oliver defended himself. "Anyway, *you're* the one who let him inside in the first place!"

"I felt bad watching him standing out in the rain!" Jessie exclaimed. "It scrambled my rational thinking!"

"It's not your fault," Isa told Jessie. Before Oliver could protest, she turned to him and said, "It's not your fault either. How could we have known what he was here for?"

Isa walked over to the end table and picked up the yellow paper, and her siblings gathered around.

"'Animals present in kitchen area,'" Hyacinth read. "'Unsanitary food-preparation conditions.'"

"Of course there were animals in the kitchen!" Jessie said. "How could we possibly keep them out of there?"

"'The home processor's license is revoked, and the license holder must reapply and submit to another inspection before resuming operations,'" Oliver read out loud. He looked up at his sisters. "What are we going to do? She has the photo shoot this Friday!"

"Why does Mama need a license to bake cookies?" Hyacinth asked.

"When you're an adult, you need a license to do everything," Isa pointed out.

"Being an adult is awful," Jessie said with the air of a thirteen-year-old who was just starting to understand the multitude and magnitude of adult problems.

"Everything?" Laney asked, skeptical. "What about marrying?"

"You need a marriage license," Isa said.

"Driving?" Laney tried.

"You need a driver's license," Jessie said.

"Painting nails?" Laney asked, holding up her hands, which she had painted purple that morning. She had forgotten to let them dry before she petted Paganini, so bits of fur were stuck in the polish.

"If people pay you to paint their nails, you need a license," Isa explained.

Oliver raised his eyebrows. "Now you're just making stuff up."

"Nope," Isa said. "I know because Allegra told me." Allegra was one of Isa's best friends. "She started a nail-painting business in the cafeteria during lunch. The principal shut it down. Apparently you have to be at least seventeen years old and have a Nail Specialty license to legally paint people's nails for pay."

"And now we know that you need a home processor's license to sell cookies," Jessie said.

Hyacinth chewed the side of her finger. "We're going to tell Mama about this, right?"

"And say what?" Oliver said. " 'Hey, we destroyed your business right before the biggest day of your life. Sorry!' "

"Maybe we can fix this before she even knows," Isa said. "The first thing we need to do is reschedule the inspection *before* the photo shoot."

"There's a number right here." Jessie pointed to the bottom of the inspection paper, then handed her phone to Isa. "You can call, pretend to be Mama, and set up another appointment."

Isa put her hands behind her back. "*You're* the one who's good with impressions."

"Ooh, do Mr. Beiderman," Laney requested. "That one is hilarious."

"Your Mr. Smiley imitation is the best," Oliver chimed in. Mr. Smiley was his friend Angie's father, and the Vanderbeekers greatly admired his Russian accent.

Jessie stared at her siblings, then said, "Fine, I'll do it." She dialed the number and put the phone on speaker. After one ring, a musical voice came through.

"Good afternoon, New York State Department of

Agriculture and Markets. My name is Natasha. How may I help you?"

"Hello," Jessie said, pitching her voice a little lower and enunciating her words more clearly than usual. "Mr. West was just here for an inspection, and there were a few, uh, items that needed addressing in order to renew my m—um, *my* home processor's license. I was hoping to correct the outstanding issues and have him reinspect the premises."

"Unfortunately, there are very few inspectors in this department," Natasha said, "and they serve the entire state. Mr. West leaves New York City this Thursday, and he is completely booked. The next time an inspector is scheduled to come to your area is . . ."

The kids heard some keys tapping.

". . . September."

"Holy smokes!" Oliver said, then clapped his hand to his mouth.

"Would September work for you?" Natasha asked pleasantly, as if talking about her plans for lunch instead of determining the fate of Mama's business.

"Um, we were hoping for this week," Jessie said. "It's super, super important. Like, life and death."

"Hmm," Natasha said. "That sounds serious." The Vanderbeekers could hear her clicking around on her computer. "He just got a cancellation for Thursday at three thirty. It's his last appointment for the day, and he asked me not to put anyone else in that slot so he could go home early. But I'll just pretend I forgot."

"Oh my gosh, that would be awesome," Jessie blurted into the phone. "Thank you!"

"No problem," Natasha said. "Tell me your last name."

"Vanderbeeker."

"You said Mr. West came by today, right? Oh, I see you in the schedule! Okay, I'll put you back into the calendar for Thursday at three thirty in the afternoon. Have a nice day, now."

"You too!" Jessie said, then clicked the phone off.

The Vanderbeekers air high-fived.

"That's one problem solved," Isa said.

"Only a thousand more problems to go," Jessie said as her phone buzzed with an incoming text message. "It's Mama," she said, then read it out loud. " 'I'll be back in ten minutes. The inspector shouldn't be there for twenty more minutes, but if he's early, be super nice to him!' "

"Tell her the inspection was rescheduled for next week, after the photo shoot," Isa told Jessie. "That way we can fix everything before she even knows about it."

Jessie glanced at Isa, then typed a brief message back. "He rescheduled for next Monday."

Mama wrote back immediately. "Great!"

Jessie typed again. "Franz knocked over a tray of your cookies. We're sorry."

Mama's message was short: "UGH."

Jessie put her phone in her pocket, then looked at her siblings. "Four days until the next inspection, five days until the photo shoot."

A boom of thunder shook the brownstone, and Oliver whistled. "If we can't fix this, we're going to have to get Mama a *huge* birthday present."

Five

Twenty minutes later, Mama arrived back home. She greeted the kids, scolded Franz, then immediately got to work making a new batch of chocolate sea salt caramel cookies. The kids closed all the curtains in case Mr. West was lurking outside and waiting to slam her with a violation and a fine.

While Mama was busy with the cookies, Isa gathered her siblings and they descended into the basement with Franz and Princess Cutie, closing the door so Mama wouldn't overhear them. Isa trailed her hands along the banister as she went downstairs, feeling the familiar grooves of the wood pressing into her fingers. This daily ritual usually filled her with peace, but today even the brownstone's comfort eluded her.

When Isa reached the bottom, she sat on a floor pillow and rubbed her temples, thinking about the mess they had gotten themselves into. Her orchestra audition was Friday morning, right before the photo shoot. They needed to save Mama's business, prepare the brownstone, and plan Mama's birthday by then, *and* Isa had to nail her audition.

Isa looked out at her siblings, who were arguing over the remaining floor pillows. Franz, in a fit of boredom a few weeks earlier, had pulled most of the stuffing from two of them, and no one wanted to be stuck with those. Overhead, white twinkle lights crisscrossed the ceiling, and garlands of silvery stars reflected their glow and shimmered in happiness at the Vanderbeekers' appearance.

Isa cleared her throat to get her siblings' attention. "Who has ideas?"

"We could give away our pets," Oliver joked. He was immediately smacked with pillows by all of his sisters except Hyacinth. Hyacinth's eyes filled with tears.

"It was a joke!" Oliver said.

"Not funny, Oliver," Hyacinth said.

"Sorry," Oliver said, chastened. "Hey, maybe we could hide the pets during the inspection. We could *say* we found new homes for them, but we'll actually just bring them to someone else's place until Mr. West leaves."

"That could work," Jessie said. "We'd have to hide all their stuff, though. Kitty litterbox, Paganini's hay box, Franz's bed—"

"Franz's toys, his leash, his food . . ." Oliver continued.

"These animals have more stuff than we do," Jessie remarked.

"But that doesn't solve the license problem," Hyacinth said. "What if Mr. West comes back later and sees all the animals? Mama would get in big trouble."

"Hmm . . . Hyacinth makes a good point," Isa said.

"Maybe Mama could bake upstairs, in Mr. Jeet and Miss Josie's apartment. Or in Mr. Beiderman's place," Jessie suggested.

"Not a bad idea," Isa said.

"Mr. Jeet has to take lots of naps," Laney announced. "Sometimes he falls asleep when he's talking to me."

"True," Isa said. "I can't see Mama wanting to impose on them."

"Mr. Beiderman has Princess Cutie," Laney added, "and she jumps up on counters and eats from his plate, and he lets her when he thinks no one is watching."

The older Vanderbeekers paused to consider this new revelation. Their parents were adamant that the kids never feed the pets table food, ever.

"This sounds like a hard problem," Laney said. "Too hard for us."

"We have to do *something*," Isa reasoned.

"It was a mistake!" Laney said.

"Yes," Isa said slowly. "But when you make a mistake, you have to fix it, right?"

"Mama usually fixes my mistakes," Laney said with a shrug.

It did seem as if Mama fixed the majority of Laney's mistakes, like the time Laney accidentally spilled nail polish on a library book (Mama paid to replace it) or the unfortunate day when Laney flushed Isa's violin rosin down the toilet (Laney still could not provide a reasonable explanation for how *that* happened). Mama had run to the music shop and bought more rosin because Isa had a concert that evening, and without rosin the bow wouldn't make a sound against the strings.

"Laney, you just had a birthday, right?" Isa said.

Laney nodded.

"Well, you're six now. When you're older, you get to do lots of new things, but you also have to be more responsible," Isa explained.

Laney frowned. "That doesn't sound like a lot of fun."

Isa sighed deeply, and Jessie stood up and gestured for her siblings to follow her. "Come on, Isa needs to practice."

"But we still have to figure out what to do about this inspection disaster," Isa said.

"I thought we decided to move the pets during the inspection," Jessie said, brushing her hands together. "Easy."

Hyacinth rubbed her stomach. "I don't feel so good about that plan. It's not solving the problem."

"It's a temporary fix," Jessie explained. "We just need to get through the photo shoot, and then we can figure out what to do next." Her cell phone buzzed, and she checked the message. "Hey, Oliver, that was Uncle Arthur. He wanted to let you know that he's not coming today. The weather is too bad to work on the treehouse."

"Ugh!" Oliver yelled as he stomped up the stairs.

Isa watched as her siblings disappeared from view. A moment later, she could hear their footsteps above, distinct in their own ways: Jessie's purposeful tread, Oliver's angry stomps, Hyacinth's quiet walk, and Laney's thumps from rolling and cartwheeling. Isa rubbed her temples. She didn't feel good about their plan to get Mama's license back, she felt bad for Oliver and his canceled treehouse plans, and her upcoming audition weighed on her as if she were carrying a backpack filled with rocks up a mountain.

Isa sat thinking about all these things, and a wave of loneliness washed over her. For so many years, she had found the solitude of the basement comforting and necessary. She had started playing the violin eight years ago, which meant thousands of trips downstairs to practice. But recently, some days felt so heavy, as if the practicing was a pointless exercise. Was she even improving? What if she got to the audition and didn't measure up?

Isa unzipped her violin case and removed the soft cloths that covered her instrument. Next to her, the radiator let out a low, comforting whistle. Isa knew the whistles would fade in a few weeks with the arrival of spring weather, and as she rubbed rosin onto her bow, she thought about how she would miss the sound.

She tuned her strings, letting the music fill the basement and wrap around her. She breathed in the notes, allowing them to roll through her lungs. She warmed up with some slow scales, letting her bow sink deep into the strings and send vibrations through the brownstone. The sound was satisfying and solid, and Isa relaxed into her practice—

Bang! Bang!

Oliver was hammering something upstairs. Sometimes he pounded nails into a large block of wood when he was mad.

Concentrate, Isa chastised herself.

Bang! Bang! Bang!

Isa took a deep breath. *You need to play through any*

situation, she lectured herself. *You're not some diva who needs utter quiet.*

Isa channeled the composer Camille Saint-Saëns, who had written the music nearly one hundred and fifty years earlier. She played the first chord of the third movement of the Violin Concerto in B Minor, remembering the advice of her teacher, Mr. Van Hooten: *Sink into the sound! Vibrate to the ends of the notes!* The radiator whistled next to her.

Bang!

This time, Isa gritted her teeth and did not stop.

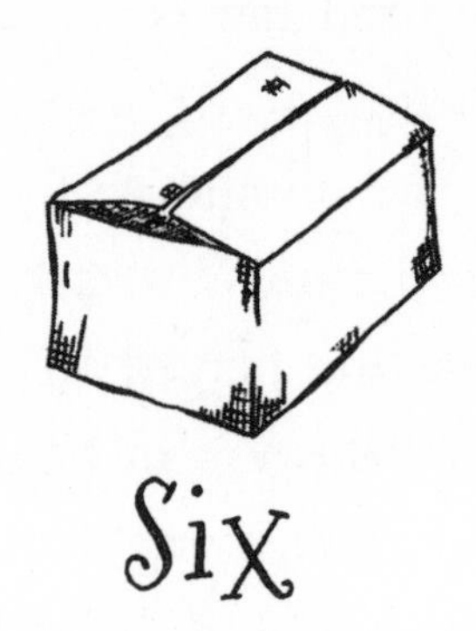

Six

While Isa was practicing, Hyacinth helped Mama finish the new batch of cookies. Laney made her way upstairs for her daily visit to Mr. Jeet and Miss Josie. She'd packed Paganini into the animal carrier and grabbed a fistful of the buttercup winterhazel that was growing in their backyard. The brownstone murmured its welcome-to-my-stairs noises—gentle creaks and sighs—as she ascended. When she got to the second floor, Laney put her ear to the door and listened. Hearing kitchen sounds, she knocked while Paganini shuffled restlessly in his carrier. Miss Josie's laugh drifted through the door, and then it opened.

"Ah, my Laney," Miss Josie said. "How nice to see you this morning." Miss Josie wore a dress with magenta flowers printed all over it, and she wrapped Laney in a bear hug—Laney had to hold the winter-hazel away from her body to keep it from getting squished. When she was released, she presented the bouquet, which Miss Josie fussed over before walking to the kitchen and filling a glass vase with water.

Laney glanced at the living room, but Mr. Jeet was missing from his usual armchair.

"Is Mr. Jeet still in bed?" Laney asked. This was unusual; both Mr. Jeet and Miss Josie rose with the sun.

"He is," Miss Josie said.

"Is he sick?" Laney asked.

Miss Josie shook her head. "Let's sit down. I want to talk to you."

Laney nodded and tried to swallow, but it was as if a little rock were lodged in her throat. She perched herself at the very edge of the couch, and before Miss Josie could say another word, Laney jumped up and blurted out, "Mr. Jeet probably needs water. I'll get him some. Water is very important. Miss Fran told me that." Miss Fran was the nurse who came to check on Mr. Jeet twice a week.

Miss Josie reached out a hand and touched Laney's elbow. "Honey, sit for a second."

Laney lowered herself back onto the couch.

"Mr. Jeet is slowing down," Miss Josie told her. "He needs more rest now."

Laney knew that, but she wished things didn't have to change. Mr. Jeet didn't talk anymore after his second stroke the previous summer, and he rarely left the apartment because stairs were difficult for him. "Does he need to go back to the doctor? Does he need more medicine?"

"Miss Fran will be coming around more to help us," Miss Josie told her. "Mr. Jeet will probably be in bed a lot more than usual."

Laney frowned. "Can I see him now?"

Miss Josie nodded, and Laney went to the kitchen to fill a glass of water for Mr. Jeet.

Laney carried the water into the small bedroom. She had never spent much time there—usually they hung out in the living room. She put the water on the bedside table next to a framed photo of Mr. Jeet, Miss Josie, and the Vanderbeekers all sitting on the outside steps of the brownstone. Laney was a baby in the photo; she was in Mr. Jeet's lap, swaddled in a blanket. Mr. Jeet was wearing a crisp striped shirt and a navy-blue bow tie.

Laney looked from the photo to the bed. Mr. Jeet seemed so small under the covers. His eyes were closed and his arms lay at his sides. Miss Josie entered the room quietly and placed Paganini's carrier next to the bed. Laney unzipped it, lifted the rabbit out, and put him next to Mr. Jeet. The old man's eyes opened, and he looked at Laney and smiled. Paganini put his front paws on Mr. Jeet's chest, and Mr. Jeet's right hand stroked the soft bunny fur. Paganini's eyes closed in delight.

Laney took Mr. Jeet's other hand and squeezed it three times. It was a sign they had determined would mean "I love you." Laney picked up his glass of water.

"Are you thirsty?" she asked.

Mr. Jeet shook his head.

"You should drink some water anyway," Laney told him. "Hydration is very important."

He closed his eyes briefly, then nodded. She lifted the glass to his mouth, and he took a few sips, then moved his head back, indicating he was finished. His eyes drifted closed again, and Paganini flattened himself onto the bed and pressed his body next to Mr. Jeet's side.

Laney watched Mr. Jeet sleep and wondered if she would ever hear his voice again. Hyacinth had once told her that when she turned eighty-six like Mr. Jeet, she probably would have used up all the words she had ever wanted to say. Laney really hoped that Mr. Jeet had not used up all of his words already. She missed his words very much.

Ten minutes later, Miss Josie came into the room and settled down in the armchair. Laney snuggled into Miss Josie's lap, and together they sat, already missing the Mr. Jeet who got dressed in a crisp shirt and bow tie every morning, the Mr. Jeet who sat in the armchair and talked to Laney about how seeds grow and why dog tails wag and where clouds come from. Even though he was lying right there, Laney felt as if she were losing her best friend.

❋ ❋ ❋

Oliver was *not* in a good mood. He was mad at the inspector for ruining Mama's business, mad at the rain for making it impossible to work on the treehouse, and mad at Uncle Arthur for canceling on him. He pounded nail after nail into the thick wood plank, stopping only when Mama put on her raincoat and got ready to leave with a new batch of chocolate sea salt caramel cookies. She leaned down and ruffled Oliver's hair, then looked into his eyes.

"Everything okay?" she asked.

Oliver shrugged.

"I'm sorry you couldn't work on the treehouse today. This weather stinks," Mama said. She pulled two cookies out of the box and handed them to him with a wink and a kiss on the forehead. "Love you."

Mama grabbed her umbrella and headed out the door, and Oliver took a bite of cookie and immediately felt the day getting better. Over at the dining room table, Jessie had three huge science books open and was jotting furiously in a notebook. Oliver could hear Isa doing scales in the basement, and Laney and Hyacinth were upstairs. Outside, the rain continued to pound against the walls and windows of the brownstone. Franz flew down the stairs and ran to the back door, whimpering.

"Hyacinth, your dog needs to go out!" Oliver called,

but Hyacinth didn't respond. Franz scratched at the door.

With a huge sigh, Oliver got up, walked to the back door, and opened it. Instead of racing out into the yard, Franz whimpered and sank to the ground.

"C'mon, Franz," Oliver said. Then he caught sight of a box—a very wet box—on the top step. He reached down to pick it up, but just before his hands connected with it, the box wobbled.

Oliver blinked, unsure whether he had imagined it.

The box shook again, and Oliver scrambled backwards. Franz howled.

"Uh, Jessie?" Oliver called.

"Yeah?" she said in a distracted, I'm-thinking-about-science way.

"Can you come here?" Oliver asked.

"No," she answered.

"Really, I think you should come here. Maybe you can use your science brain to help me figure out what could make a box move on its own."

Jessie's head popped up, just as Laney and Hyacinth appeared, gliding down the stairs wrapped in long pieces of silk over their clothes.

"Look at our beautiful dresses!" Laney exclaimed, spinning around.

"That box is moving!" Oliver shouted, pointing at the door.

Laney and Hyacinth stopped in their tracks.

Oliver didn't budge from his spot a few yards from the open door. He pointed. "Over there."

His sisters looked at the box. It was as still as a box could be.

"Are you sure, Oliver?" Jessie said.

"It just moved. I saw it," Oliver insisted.

Dutifully, Jessie, Hyacinth, and Laney looked again at the box.

It didn't move.

"Don't take your eyes off it," Oliver instructed.

Jessie went to the box and tapped it with her foot. She turned around to face her siblings, her hands spread out beside her. "See? It's a normal box, Oliver."

Then the box jiggled, all on its own.

Laney and Hyacinth screamed. Franz lifted his head and howled. The brownstone creaked ominously.

Jessie jumped, tripped over a kitchen stool, and looked back at the box. "What? What happened?"

No one answered, because they were too busy leaping for safety. Laney and Hyacinth slid behind the kitchen island, Franz following closely. Oliver jumped over the couch and huddled behind it. Jessie, still not sure what they had all seen, was so alarmed by their reactions that she fled toward the basement to get Isa.

Footsteps thundered up the steps and Isa burst through the door, nearly squashing Jessie as she flung it open. "Is something on fire?" she asked, breathless.

Jessie pointed toward the back door. "There's something alive in there."

"Really?" Isa said, walking toward the box.

This time, with all the Vanderbeekers' eyes on it, the box moved again.

"Ahhh!" yelled Laney, Oliver, Jessie, and Hyacinth. Franz howled.

"There's *definitely* something alive in there," Isa said matter-of-factly. "Franz, quiet!" She walked right up to the box, nudged it with her shoe, then leaned down to open the top flap.

"Isa, wait!" Hyacinth yelled.

But Isa didn't listen.

Seven

Isa was pretty sure there was nothing in the box to worry about, but as she leaned down and reached for the flaps, she saw something bump against the side. Then the wet cardboard split in two from what appeared to be a vicious claw.

She glanced at her siblings, their faces a mixture of worry and dread.

"Don't be a hero!" Jessie called to Isa.

Isa turned back around and lifted the flap. Instantly a black-and-white clawed paw reached out and attached to her hand.

"Ouch!" Isa said. It was like getting four shots at once.

"Isa! Are you okay?" Jessie yelled from her spot by the basement door.

"Yeah, but—ouch!" Another claw—this one gray—latched on.

"What is it?" Hyacinth asked, her arm around Franz's neck.

Isa tried to detach the claws. "I think they're—ouch!—kittens."

"Kittens!" exclaimed Laney, Hyacinth, Oliver, and Jessie all at once, approaching the box.

Isa successfully detached the claws, then lifted the other flap so they could see inside. Sure enough, five kittens the size of grapefruits were scrambling all over one another. Franz galloped over and sniffed around.

The five Vanderbeeker kids oohed and aahed over the kittens, a sad-looking bunch with patchy hair and prominent ribs. Hyacinth ran to get some towels to dry them off, and Franz stuck his head over the edge of the box, then pulled it out abruptly when a kitten batted his nose. He backed up five paces and barked.

"They're so skinny," Laney observed. She had already picked up a tuxedo kitten and was snuggling it under her chin.

“Don’t touch them!” Oliver said. “They might have rabies.” He glanced back at Isa in alarm. “Maybe you have rabies right now!”

“I didn’t get bitten. Anyway, I thought only dogs got rabies,” Isa said. “Franz, shhh!”

Franz did not stop barking.

“What’s rabies?” Laney asked, kissing the top of the kitten’s head.

“It’s a disease that makes you foam at the mouth. It looks like your mouth is full of toothpaste bubbles,” Oliver explained, yelling to be heard over Franz. “And cats can definitely get rabies. I read about it in a book.”

Laney hastily returned the kitten to the box, where it mewled and stood on its hind legs, begging to be picked up again.

“But transmission only happens if the kittens were exposed to wild animals,” Jessie said.

“They look like wild animals,” Oliver commented.

“Poor sweethearts,” Hyacinth said, trying to calm Franz down by scratching his head. “I think they need to see the veterinarian. Franz, hush!”

“You always think that,” Oliver said. “You worry too much.”

"Isa should go to the doctor, to see if she has rabies," Hyacinth added, looking at her sister as if she expected Isa to turn into a werewolf at any moment.

"I don't have rabies!" Isa said. "It's a scratch, not a bite." She wasn't sure about the whole rabies thing, but the kittens did look like they needed to see a veterinarian.

"Wait a second," Jessie said. "Forget rabies. We have bigger problems."

"A bigger problem than *rabies*?" Oliver said.

"The inspection?" Jessie reminded him. "The photo shoot? Saving Mama's business? We need to be clearing the apartment of animals, not adding more."

The Vanderbeekers fell quiet, until Isa finally took a breath. "Let's tackle this one step at a time. First we should take the kittens to Dr. Singh. She'll know what to do."

❋ ❋ ❋

The Vanderbeekers decided that the safest way to transport the kittens to Dr. Singh was to use their trusty Radio Flyer wagon. Jessie moved the kittens to a dry box and put the box in the wagon; then she ordered everyone to put on their raincoats and boots. Hyacinth leashed up Franz and draped a bright yellow doggie raincoat over him, because she was certain he would not want to miss a visit to Dr. Singh. Unlike most dogs, Franz loved going to the vet. He was a favorite there, and the office manager and vet technicians spoiled him with dog treats.

The Vanderbeekers set off down the block with the box of kittens, Franz, and the three umbrellas they found under the shoe rack by the front door. A tarp was thrown over the kitten box to keep them dry, and they sloshed their way to the veterinarian's office, where they were well known. At least once a week, the siblings went there after school so they could hang out with the hospitalized or lonely animals that were being boarded. Laney, who refused to use an umbrella, jumped into every puddle until all of her siblings scolded her to stop because she kept splashing everyone's pants.

"We'll take the kittens back home after Dr. Singh makes them feel better, right?" Laney asked, brushing her wet hair away from her face.

"That would be a negative," Oliver said. "Remember the inspection?"

"No more animals," Isa reminded her, huddled under an umbrella with Jessie. "Dr. Singh takes in rescues. We'll give the kittens to her, and she'll take great care of them until they get homes."

Laney pouted. "We could take even *better* care of them at our home."

Hyacinth quietly agreed and pulled the hood of her raincoat closer around her face.

"Does anyone else feel like this is totally strange?" Jessie asked a moment later. "A box of famished kittens arrives at our doorstep right after we get an inspection, and Mama's home license gets revoked because we have animals in the brownstone. Who left them? And why? And is there a connection to the inspection?"

Isa spoke up. "I can't imagine it's connected to the inspection. No one else knew about it."

"Mr. West knew about it," Oliver said ominously.

Jessie snorted. "Mr. West wouldn't leave a box of kittens at our door just to sabotage us."

Hyacinth thought about Mr. West and his obvious aversion to animals. "Maybe he doesn't like animals because he's never had a pet."

"Some people don't have pets?" Laney asked, befuddled.

"Mr. West needs to know the love of an animal," Hyacinth announced.

"Oh no," Jessie said. "Don't get any big ideas."

"What big ideas?" Hyacinth asked.

Jessie narrowed her eyes at Hyacinth. "Those let's-leave-a-kitten-outside-Mr.-Beiderman's-door ideas."

Hyacinth shrugged. "It worked, didn't it?" She was referring to something that had happened a year and a half earlier, when the Vanderbeekers were trying to convince Mr. Beiderman to renew their lease. Hyacinth had left a kitten outside Mr. Beiderman's door in an effort to melt their neighbor's frozen heart.

"I still think it was brilliant," Oliver said. "It definitely tipped the scales in our favor."

Isa looked at Hyacinth. "You are *not* going to give Mr. West a kitten, okay?"

Hyacinth didn't reply.

Isa put a hand on Hyacinth's shoulder and leaned down so they were eye to eye. Franz jumped up and tried to lick Isa's face.

"I need you to say out loud that you are not going to give Mr. West a kitten," Isa said, gently pushing Franz's face away from hers.

Hyacinth crossed her fingers behind her back and looked at Isa. "I promise I will not give Mr. West a kitten."

"She's crossing her fingers behind her back," Jessie said.

Hyacinth glared at Jessie, uncrossed her fingers, put them out in front of her, then repeated her oath.

Relieved, Isa straightened and rolled the wagon to the entrance of Central Harlem Animal Hospital on Adam Clayton Powell Jr. Boulevard between 143rd and 144th Streets. It was sandwiched between a bodega and a preschool.

Hyacinth opened the door, and the little bell that was tied to the doorknob jingled, which set off a cacophony of barks, yells, yowls, and meows. The Vanderbeekers filed inside and stood in the lobby, dripping. Franz woofed and gave a vigorous shake.

"Holy smokes, it's loud in here," Isa said.

Dr. Singh raced past them in a blur, carrying a white dog in her arms. The vet technician had his arm around a woman who appeared to be the frantic pet owner and was guiding her into one of the examination rooms. Miss Ethel, the receptionist, was on the phone talking to someone in a serious tone.

"What's going on?" Hyacinth asked Isa. She had never seen the office in such a state of chaos. Sometimes when they stopped by, Dr. Singh would be on her afternoon break and her assistant would give them steaming chai tea served in tiny metal cups. Dr. Singh liked to show them photos of animals she had recently operated on.

"Look at these gorgeous sutures," she would brag.

Hyacinth personally did not like looking at the post-surgery photos, but for some inexplicable reason, Oliver, Jessie, and Laney loved it.

Miss Ethel put the phone down, then gave the Vanderbeekers a harried smile. "Sorry, guys, but it's not a good time to visit. Dr. Singh has two emergency patients and is going into surgery in twenty minutes. Can you come back tomorrow?"

"We wanted her to look at these kittens," Hyacinth said. "They showed up outside our door this morning. We don't know if they're sick or not."

"We were hoping Dr. Singh could check them out and then keep them here for adoption," Jessie added.

Franz howled in agreement.

Miss Ethel's face softened at the sound of Franz's voice. "How's my Franz?" she cooed, reaching into her drawer and pulling out a bag of treats. She stepped around the desk, and Franz's tail hitched up to 125 wpm, or wags per minute, as she fed him a dog biscuit. Then, realizing that the Vanderbeekers were all soaking wet, she pulled a few towels from the closet and passed them around before checking out the kittens.

"They are precious," Miss Ethel said, "but we're already housing ten kittens for adoption. I can see if the new vet tech is here to give you some pointers on taking care of them, but we won't be able to take them in right now."

There was a stunned silence.

"But what will we do with them?" Oliver asked at the same time Laney exclaimed, "Yay! We can keep them!"

"We really *can't* keep them," Isa said, using a towel to dry her hair.

"I don't know what to tell you," Miss Ethel said.

The Vanderbeekers looked at one another in resignation.

"Our new vet tech just started a few days ago, and she's a little . . . well, you'll see." Miss Ethel picked up the phone, punched some numbers, and then spoke into the mouthpiece. "Oh good, you're here. Can you come upstairs?" She hung up, then raised her eyebrows at the Vanderbeekers. "Get ready to meet Cassandra."

Eight

"Oh my gosh, Miss Ethel! Are you really letting me *treat* patients? I am *so* excited! Are these the little sweethearts? Oh, they are *so* cute! Wait, can you take a picture of me with them? My parents are going to freak out!"

The Vanderbeekers stared at Cassandra. She had hair the color of a sunset, and she spoke as if she had just gulped down five cups of coffee. Isa took the offered cell phone and dutifully snapped some photos of Cassandra and the kittens.

Cassandra flipped through the photos, then started pressing the phone keys with her fingers. "These are awesome. My parents are going to be so proud. My first patients! Miss Ethel, can you believe it?"

Miss Ethel shooed Cassandra away with a flick of her wrist. "Go downstairs, please. Dr. Singh doesn't need to be tripping over you right now."

Cassandra beamed a smile as bright as a rainbow at Miss Ethel. "I'll make you proud! Don't you worry! Okay, kids, follow me!"

The Vanderbeekers followed Cassandra downstairs, leaving a trail of rainwater behind them. Laney kept trying to insert a comment about Cassandra's hair, but for once, she couldn't get a word in edgewise.

"Oh, aren't they precious?" Cassandra cooed. "Now, they look a bit skinny. Are you feeding them enough? Oh! That one may have coughed. Maybe kennel cough. Hmm . . ."

"We found them outside our apartment this morning," Jessie said hastily while Cassandra took a breath.

"Abandoned kittens! And in this terrible weather!" Cassandra exclaimed. "What is wrong with this world! Thank you for bringing them in. It's very important to treat any issues right away. 'An ounce of prevention is worth a pound of cure,' as someone—I have no idea who!—once said. What a wise person, right?"

"We're worried they have rabies!" Laney blurted out, finally finding a moment to insert her thoughts.

Cassandra squinted at the kittens. "Rabies? Why do you think that? Well, I guess it *is* the main fear people have about abandoned animals. Unwarranted, let me tell you. Sort of like how people are afraid of sharks even though they only kill, like, one person every two years. Come into the examination room, quick, quick! Oops, I need to get my stethoscope. My aunt bought me a new one when I got into veterinary school. Okay! I think I'm set." Cassandra gave her phone to Isa again. "Can you take a photo of me using my stethoscope on this adorable kitten? Oh my gosh, my parents are going to flip! I bet this photo will go viral. I mean, kitten videos get the most views of any animal video, did you know that? Here, can you lay this towel down on the table?"

Laney took the towel and put it over the metal table while Isa snapped a few more photos of Cassandra examining the kittens.

"This is so cool! Who wants to hear the heartbeat?"

Laney was by her side so quick that if you blinked, you would have missed her moving. Cassandra put the stethoscope to her ears. "Isn't that the most beautiful sound in the world?" she asked, her voice hushed. "That's her heart pumping. The sound of life."

Laney heard a steady thump and whoosh through the stethoscope, and for a second she almost felt transported into the kitten's little heart.

"Isn't life a miracle?" Cassandra said as she continued examining the kittens. She shined a light into their eyes ("Ooh, Isa, can you take a photo of me doing that?"), felt their tummies ("Feels good to me!"), and looked inside their ears ("No ear mites!"). She took their temperatures and checked for fleas ("I cannot *wait* to tell my parents about this!").

Finally Cassandra put all her veterinary tools down. "These guys look great! I know you're worried about rabies—everyone is—but honestly? It is so rare to have rabid animals roaming around New York City. It's not like the Great Wilderness, am I right?" She laughed at her own joke. "Last year there was only one reported rabid animal in all of Manhattan, and that was a raccoon. Anyhow, I estimate these adorable munchkins are ten weeks old. See their eyes? See the amount of fur they have?

"Okay, here's the plan. I'm going to give them all vaccinations. Dr. Singh won't charge you for that because these are rescue animals, and she likes to give the first checkup and vaccinations for free. Isn't Dr. Singh the coolest? She's my hero. Maybe one day after I finish vet school I'll join her practice and I can put my diploma up on the wall right next to hers.

"All right, all you need to do is fatten these kittens up. Isn't that fun? It's much better to help animals gain weight than lose weight." She paused to glance at Franz. His tummy hung low to the ground.

Franz looked up at her with his droopy eyes. Laney thought he was trying to hypnotize her into giving him a treat.

Cassandra opened a can of kitten food and spooned it into a long, low dish. The kittens immediately scampered to it and started eating. Laney watched them, and it gave her the best feeling in the world, even better than when she wore her favorite puffy skirt and silky top, rainbow socks, and sparkly high-tops all at once.

"I don't think you'll have any problem with them

eating," Cassandra said. "I'll send you home with some kitten food. Feed these precious sweethearts twice a day," she continued, "and they'll be all set!"

"Whoa, whoa," Jessie said, putting her hands up. "We can't *keep* these animals."

Cassandra's eyes grew wide. "We already have ten kittens we're trying to get adopted. No room here; no, ma'am. If any of them have trouble eating, bring them back immediately. But I suspect they'll gain weight in no time. I want to see them for another checkup in two weeks, okay?"

"We *really* can't keep them," Jessie insisted, avoiding her siblings' glares. "Our mom's business is at stake. What should we do?"

Cassandra's smile flatlined, and Laney was struck by how sad she suddenly felt. "The only thing I can suggest is that you bring them to the local shelter," Cassandra said. "There's an Animal Care Center not too far from here." Cassandra wrote the address on a piece of paper and handed it to Jessie. "But I hope you can take care of them for a little bit and find them homes. That's really the best way. The kittens will become nice and socialized around you, and then it will be easier to get them adopted. Plus they don't have to live in cages, which is so depressing."

The Vanderbeekers nodded and thanked Cassandra for the supplies. Cassandra insisted on a photo with all of them, each holding a kitten ("I'm totally posting this on social media!"), before saying goodbye.

Laney turned back as they went up the stairs and looked at Cassandra. She was now picking up a dog from a kennel and murmuring in his ear, and Laney decided then and there that when she grew up, she wanted to be a veterinarian. And when that day came, she was going to be *exactly* like Cassandra.

Nine

The Vanderbeekers stood outside Central Harlem Animal Hospital, getting rained on all over again. Four kittens were back in the wagon, the tarp draped over them. Laney had the fifth kitten snuggled against her chest inside her raincoat.

"I guess we have to go to the animal shelter," Jessie said, looking at Isa for confirmation.

"I guess," Isa said. "I feel bad, but we can't take care of them right now. We need to save Mama's business." Her phone pinged, and she glanced at it, then looked at Oliver. "That was Uncle Arthur. He decided to come over anyway and wants to know if you'd be up for helping him build bookcases."

Oliver's eyes brightened. "Tell him yes!" he said, and started running in the direction of the brownstone.

"Oliver, wait!" Jessie said. Oliver did not slow down. "Isa, you go with him. You can practice, Oliver can work on the bookshelves, and I'll take Laney and Hyacinth to the shelter to drop off the kittens."

Hyacinth choked back a sob at the thought of leaving the kittens. Franz sat next to her, his big head leaning against her knee.

"I can't let you go to the shelter by yourself," Isa said to Jessie. "Don't you have a science project to do?"

"I've got all week," Jessie said with a shrug. "Plus Orlando and I need to work on it together. Hey, Oliver, wait up!"

Oliver turned around, his hair a wet mop around him. "Come on!" he yelled.

"Fine," Isa told Jessie. "Take the umbrella, okay?" She handed the umbrella to Jessie before peeking under the tarp at the kittens. She whispered, "Have a good life, little guys," before running to catch up with Oliver.

Meanwhile, Hyacinth felt like a balloon that had

deflated, and she tried to keep her tears inside instead of rolling down her cheeks.

Jessie grimaced and picked up the wagon handle. "Let's do this," she muttered, then led the way to the Animal Care Center, which was about a mile away on 122nd Street between Adam Clayton Powell Jr. Boulevard and Frederick Douglass Boulevard.

Although Harlem lacked football fields and running tracks, hiking trails and great big open spaces, the Vanderbeekers were A+ walkers; they could walk for miles on the city streets without getting tired. Franz, on the other hand, started fading around 135th Street. When he lay down in a big puddle and refused to get back up again, Jessie and Hyacinth heaved him into the wagon and continued on their way. There he sat, alert and howling at ambulances passing by and greeting dogs and kids with a prick of his ears and a wag of his tail.

Hyacinth did not get a good feeling when they turned onto 122nd Street and headed east toward the address Cassandra had given her. Nearly half the buildings were shrouded in black netting, and rusty metal scaffolding blocked all the sunlight. The wretched weather made the block seem even gloomier.

Laney, who had carried the tuxedo kitten inside her raincoat the entire way from 143rd Street, was getting more and more anxious. She kept murmuring things to herself and looking around furtively, as if she were planning to temporarily stash her kitten somewhere on the street and hoping Jessie wouldn't notice a kitten was missing when she turned over the box.

They arrived at the shelter, a gray building with posters in all the windows that said SAVE A LIFE! ADOPT TODAY! with adorable kittens and dogs with big, sad eyes.

"I don't want to go in there," Laney said.

"We don't have a choice," Jessie said grimly. She shook out the umbrella, grabbed Laney's elbow, and marched inside.

Behind the reception desk, a man with a name tag that said HI! I'M FRANKIE! ASK ME ABOUT ADOPTION TODAY! greeted them with a giant smile. "Are you interested in adopting today?" he asked.

"No," Jessie said, shaking raindrops from the sleeves of her coat.

Franz woofed in agreement.

Frankie's face fell. "You're surrendering your beautiful dog?"

Hyacinth put a protective arm around Franz and glared at Frankie. "We would *never* give away Franz!"

Frankie put his hands up in surrender. "I'm sorry. You can't even imagine the pets that get abandoned here."

Laney and Jessie relented. "It's okay," they said.

Hyacinth refused to look at him.

"These kittens were left outside our door this morning." Jessie picked up the box from the wagon and put it on the reception desk. Frankie peered inside. "There was no mother cat around," Jessie continued, "and we took them to our vet, but she can't take them in, and Cassandra said the kittens are about ten weeks old and can't take care of themselves yet."

"Aren't they cute?" Laney asked.

"Then they gave us your address and said we could bring the animals here," Jessie finished.

Frankie looked at the kittens. "Well, *technically* we can take them in because they're strays. For most owner surrenders, we require people to make an appointment, meet with a counselor and a veterinarian, then pay a fee if they do end up leaving the animal here."

"Owner surrenders?" Hyacinth said. "That's terrible."

"Our shelter is overcrowded right now, so you should know that the outcome would be much better for these beautiful little creatures if you found a home for them on your own."

"We can't bring them home," Jessie explained. "We've already messed up Mama's life enough."

Frankie gave a disappointed sigh. "If you're certain you want to leave them here, then come with me."

"We're certain," Jessie said at the same time Hyacinth said, "I'm *not* certain."

Frankie put the box back into the wagon with Franz, and he pulled it down the hallway with the Vanderbeekers following him. After walking for a minute, a steady rumbling grew louder and louder, until Hyacinth could distinguish individual barks, howls, and snarls. Then Frankie opened a door, and the whoosh of sound reminded Hyacinth of the time they went to an air show and the Thunderbirds roared above them with their huge engines.

Row upon row of cages filled the room, and in each one were animals. There were cages with dozens of puppies scrambling over one another, and there were big dogs barking and jumping at the doors. But even worse were the dogs lying down in the cages, their heads resting on their paws, their sad eyes roving but empty of hope. Hyacinth had the feeling that those dogs had been there for a long, long time.

After walking through that room, they entered a new room dominated by hisses, meows, and howls. This was the cat room. Again, cages and cages of animals.

"How many cats are here?" Hyacinth asked.

Frankie looked at a chart on the wall over Hyacinth's shoulder. "Three hundred and four," he said. "And with your five, I guess it'll be three hundred and nine."

Hyacinth swallowed. "How long will it take for them to be adopted?"

"About five cats are adopted every day," Frankie said.

"What happens to the cats that don't get adopted?" Jessie asked.

Frankie looked at Jessie; then his eyes skidded over to Hyacinth and Laney. "Well, they—you know."

The Vanderbeekers stared back at Frankie, not speaking.

Frankie tried again. "You know when a pet gets really old and sick? And the veterinarian gives them a shot and they go to sleep forever?"

"You mean the pets get euthanized," Hyacinth said flatly. "We had to do that with our old cat when I was four years old."

"I know all about that," Laney said. "Frances's cat had kidney cancer and got really sick and had to be euthanized."

"Exactly," Frankie said. He looked very relieved that he did not have to explain euthanasia to them. "The cats that don't get adopted after a while get euthanized."

"Even if they're not sick?" Hyacinth asked him.

"Even if they're not sick," Frankie repeated. "If we can't find homes for them, it's the only thing we can do. I wish we could find all of these animals homes, but there's just too many of them."

"At least these kittens are super cute," Jessie said, but Hyacinth could tell Jessie's determination to leave the animals was wavering. "Who could say no to them?"

"All right," Frankie said, pointing to a small room with an examination table in it. "You can leave them here. The vet will check them, and if they're healthy they'll get processed and then made available for adoption."

"Cassandra already gave them their shots," Jessie told him. She pulled the vaccination records from her back pocket and gave them to Frankie.

"That's great," Frankie said. "I'll do the best I can with these little guys." He looked at Laney. "Is that the fifth kitten?"

Laney didn't respond.

"Yes," Jessie answered for her. "Come on, Laney." She gently unzipped Laney's jacket, lifted out the warm kitten, and put her into the box. Laney started to cry. Franz howled.

"Okay, let's go," Jessie said abruptly, turning around and grabbing Laney with one hand and the handle of the wagon with the other.

"I'll walk you out," Frankie said.

Grimly, Jessie marched a sniffling Hyacinth and a sobbing Laney out of the examination room, through the room with the three hundred and four cats, and then to the dog room. A fresh round of barking started up at the sight of Frankie, Jessie, Hyacinth, Laney, and Franz.

Hyacinth looked at the rows of cages, the hundreds of animals waiting for homes. More tears filled her eyes, and she wiped them with the hem of her jacket.

"Maybe we'll find homes for them soon," Frankie said, trying to cheer the girls up.

No one replied.

"It's not such a bad place," Frankie continued. "There are lots of great volunteers, and I'll check on the kittens during my breaks."

Suddenly, in the middle of the dog room, Jessie braked, and Hyacinth and Laney bumped into her back. "I can't do this," she said. She swiveled and, without looking at her sisters, marched back through the dog room and back through the cat room. Franz bounced along in the wagon and howled at the animals, followed by Laney and Hyacinth, who had to jog to keep up. Jessie went straight back into the examination room, where someone in a lab coat was looking in the box and saying, "Oh, how adorable!"

"Sorry," Jessie said. "We forgot something." She picked up the box of kittens and put it back in the wagon next to Franz. She pulled the wagon back out of the room. For the fourth time, they rolled past the cats and the dogs, then through the reception area and out the door. Finally, Jessie stopped.

"What have I done?" she muttered, leaning down to put her hands on her knees and taking deep breaths.

Hyacinth knew Jessie wasn't much of a hugger, but she couldn't help it. She wrapped her arms around her big sister and hugged her with all her might.

Ten

Before the home processor's license debacle, Oliver had been feeling really good about spring vacation. He had planned to help clean up the brownstone for the photo shoot, of course, but mostly he wanted to work on the treehouse with Uncle Arthur.

The treehouse was a yearlong dream in the making. A platform had been installed many years ago, but it had no walls yet, which made it uninhabitable in the winter. Also, Mama refused to entertain the idea of Oliver sleeping in the treehouse, as she worried he would topple over the edge and break his neck.

With the help of his friends Angie, Jimmy L, and Herman, he had drawn up the best blueprints in the world. The planned treehouse had multiple levels plus a balcony, spy holes, a full wall of bookshelves, a twisty slide down, a built-in bench with storage underneath (including a false bottom so he could hide junk food), and a garret to be used as a reading nook.

Uncle Arthur had had to nix many of Oliver's ideas, including the slide and the garret, but the bookshelves, the built-in bench (with false bottom), and the balcony stayed. They were even going to put in real windows, which Uncle Arthur had purchased for Oliver's Christmas gift a few months earlier, along with a card that said, "Coming This April: The Treehouse of Your Dreams." Uncle Arthur had taken three whole days off during Oliver's spring break to work on it with him. The first day had been a bust, what with the weather, and Oliver worried that two days would not be enough to finish it.

It had taken them a couple of hours to build two bookcases today, and now that they were done, Oliver sat at the kitchen island, picking at a splinter wedged in his finger. Mama was back from delivering the chocolate sea salt caramel cookies to the library, and the plate of extra cookies on the kitchen counter was mocking him. Despite his promising that he would set

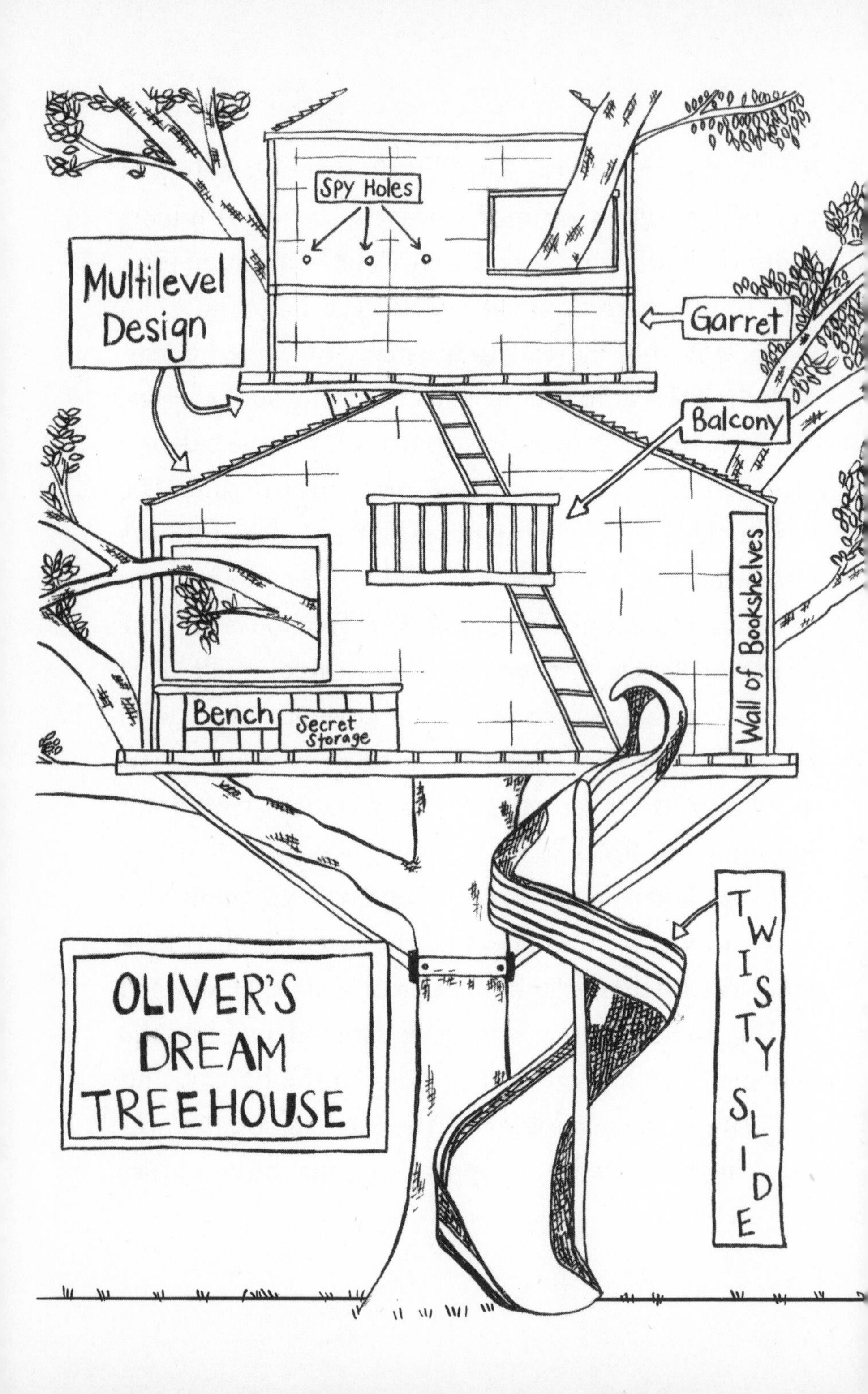
Spy Holes
Multilevel Design
Garret
Balcony
Wall of Bookshelves
Bench
Secret Storage
OLIVER'S DREAM TREEHOUSE
TWISTY SLIDE

the table *and* load the dishwasher that night, Mama did not let him have even one little cookie. She wanted to save them for dessert, and she handed him a cup of carrots instead.

Mama was cooking more than usual tonight because they were having Mega Family Dinner Night, meaning the extra leaf of the dinner table had to be inserted into the dining room table to make room for Mr. Jeet, Miss Josie, their grandnephew Orlando, Uncle Arthur, and Auntie Harrigan. Mr. Beiderman had told them he'd be back from his trip by dessert, which Oliver thought was convenient timing.

Oliver crunched on a carrot while Mama bustled around, tossing spices into the soup pot. He loved watching her in the kitchen; she always seemed to be doing ten things at once. In addition to the soup, rice was steaming in a cooker, and water was boiling for tea in anticipation of Auntie Harrigan's and Miss Josie's arrivals. Mama was checking the dinner rolls while humming along with the violin piece Isa was working on down in the basement. When the music stopped, a burst of applause drifted upstairs. Isa's friend Allegra had stopped by to hang out and was in the basement listening.

A few minutes later, Mama went upstairs to take a shower, and Isa and Allegra emerged from the basement. They each grabbed a carrot from Oliver's cup, which he was only too happy to share. He was finishing up his own carrot when the front door of the brownstone banged open. Franz bounded inside and ran straight for his food bowl in case it had mysteriously gotten filled in his absence.

"We're home!" Laney called. "Uncle Arthur, are you here?"

"I'm here!" replied Uncle Arthur. He was tossing a salad. Laney's feet pounded on the ground and she launched herself into his arms. "How's my best girl?" he asked.

"Guess what we have?" she asked him.

"Wait! I can explain!" Jessie called from the front door.

"They were going to euthanize them," Hyacinth said, entering the kitchen with an armful of library books.

"Euthanize what?" Uncle Arthur and Allegra said at the same time.

Isa paled. "Please don't tell me you—"

Jessie entered, holding a box.

"Oh no," Isa and Oliver moaned.

Hyacinth held up her books. "We stopped by the library and checked out every single book about cats!"

"The kittens are back!" Laney declared.

* * *

Oliver and Isa were looking at Jessie as if she were a criminal. Even though Jessie knew she shouldn't get attached to the kittens, she couldn't stop watching them. They were sleepy from their wagon trip and lay in a pile in the center of the box, their eyes squeezed shut, their chests moving up and down in that sweet kitten breathing rhythm. She balanced the box on her left forearm and against her chest, and she used her right hand to touch the gray kitten's forehead. It was almost time to feed them. When she looked up to check the kitchen clock, Isa, Uncle Arthur, Allegra, Oliver, and Hyacinth were all staring at her.

"What?" Jessie said.

There was a brief silence; then Isa spoke up. "I've never seen you be so . . ."

"Tender?" Oliver suggested.

"Maternal?" Allegra suggested.

Jessie frowned. "I like animals."

Hyacinth leaned down to pet Franz and hummed, one of her habits when she didn't believe what someone else was saying.

Isa pointed to the box. "What happened to the shelter? You know we can't have more animals here."

Hyacinth and Laney piped up, defending Jessie.

"It was terrible there!" Hyacinth said. "There were hundreds of animals in cages, and they were all barking or mad or sad. The guy working there said that not many get adopted, so they have to kill some of them because there are too many!"

"I wanted to adopt all of them, not leave the kittens there," Laney said.

"It was really depressing," Jessie added. "It's almost like animals are sent there to be euthanized. We had no choice."

"Well, what are we going to do now?" said Isa. "We're supposed to get rid of all animal evidence by Thursday morning!"

"Why Thursday morning?" Uncle Arthur and Allegra asked in unison.

"Oh, we, um—" Jessie said.

"See, what happened was—" Isa said.

"We're trying to fix—" Oliver said.

"It wasn't on purpose," Hyacinth said.

"We messed up bigtime," Laney finished.

Uncle Arthur's eyebrows rose. "You know what? Never mind. I need to maintain my innocence when you kids get in trouble with your parents. I'm going to fix a leaky faucet. Let me know when it's time for dinner." Uncle Arthur picked up his toolbox and headed into the ground-floor bathroom.

Allegra looked at Isa. "Can someone tell me what's going on?"

Quickly, Isa explained the situation to her friend.

"I wish you could bring the animals to our place," Allegra said, "but you know how my parents are." Allegra's apartment was like a museum, and whenever Jessie went over there, she was afraid she would bump into a piece of art and be responsible for thousands of dollars' worth of damage.

"It's okay," Isa told her. "We're going to ask Mr. Jeet and Miss Josie if Franz, George Washington, and Paganini can stay with them during the inspection.

Our backup plan is Mr. Beiderman. But adding five kittens . . . I don't know."

"Mr. Jeet isn't feeling so good," Laney reported. "Miss Josie said he's tired."

"I don't think we should bring the animals there," Hyacinth said. "It's too much for them."

"Hyacinth, will you ask Mr. Beiderman if he can take the animals on Thursday during the inspection?" Isa asked.

Hyacinth nodded.

"*And* we need to find out who left these kittens," Oliver said. "How can we do that?"

"It's Mr. West," Laney proclaimed. "He doesn't like us."

Hyacinth shook her head. "I don't think Mr. West would do that. He already took away Mama's license. Why would he bother leaving kittens?"

Oliver's eyes widened. "But maybe he saw that we rescheduled the appointment and he wants to sabotage us!"

Isa and Jessie were skeptical.

"Maybe it's not someone who hates us," Isa mused.

"Maybe it's some stranger who didn't want to keep kittens around and left them at some random person's door. In any case, we need to find homes for these kitties, pronto. They need to be out of here before the inspection."

"Aww," said Hyacinth, Laney, and Jessie.

Isa glared at Jessie. "Really? You too?"

"What?" Jessie said. "They're growing on me."

Allegra snapped her fingers. "Listen up, people. I'll come over tomorrow morning and we can make adoption flyers for the kittens. You can post them around the neighborhood."

"That would be awesome!" Isa said. "You are the best artist."

"Can you draw the kittens on the flyers?" Laney asked.

"Girl, kittens are my specialty," Allegra said.

"But not the tuxedo cat, because I want to keep that one," Laney added.

"Don't listen to her," Jessie said. "After you're done, we can go to the library and make copies and put them up around the neighborhood."

"Did you hear that?" Laney announced to the kittens. "Allegra is going to draw you!"

"I've gotta go," Allegra said, grabbing her bag. "I'll be back tomorrow."

"Stay for dinner," Isa said.

"I wish," Allegra told her. "Mom and Dad have the night off and want to have dinner with me." Allegra's parents were both pediatricians, and most of the time one or both of them were working or on call. She slipped out the door with a wave.

The kittens were awake and tumbling all over one another. Jessie let them out of the box, and George Washington observed them from a high bookshelf, his tail swishing in displeasure. Franz and Paganini, however, were elated at the visitors. They lay in the middle of the mayhem, content to have the kittens scurrying over them.

Footsteps sounded on the stairs, and Mama's voice drifted down. "Let's organize! We've got dinner guests arriving in thirty minutes!"

Before Jessie or Isa could stop her, Laney ran up the stairs to meet Mama. "We got five new kittens today!"

Mama froze. "What did you say?"

Jessie stood up and smiled her best smile. "Don't worry, Mama. We've got everything under control."

❋ ❋ ❋

Hyacinth could tell that Mama didn't know what to say, because she kept opening her mouth but no words were coming out.

"We tried to bring them to the shelter," Jessie told her, "but all the homeless animals were so sad, we couldn't leave them!"

"We'll find homes for them this week, we promise," Hyacinth said. "Allegra is making flyers!"

In the end, Mama succumbed to the little felines. The kittens, understanding that their fates were in Mama's hands, put on a show for her. They nuzzled her ankles, batted at the laces of her sneakers, and purred when she stroked their foreheads.

"You have to find homes for them," Mama finally said. "*Before* the photo shoot."

"Yes, of course," the kids chorused.

"No trying to convince me that we need more pets in this house," Mama warned them. "We're not adopting any of them."

"Right, yes," they responded.

Mama shook her head. "It's never boring being your mom."

The Vanderbeeker kids puffed up with pride, and Mama couldn't help smiling at them. "Come on, let's get dinner on the table."

Eleven

Oliver was pulling out extra folding chairs from the closet when the doorbell rang. Franz howled his way to the door, and Laney shrieked with happiness after she let in Auntie Harrigan, who swooped in, gave out hugs and lemon drops, and exclaimed over the kittens.

Papa came home from work a few moments later, froze when he saw the box of kittens, then breathed a sigh of relief when everyone assured him this was a temporary thing.

"So that means I can stop calculating the cost of providing food and veterinary care to an additional five animals?" he said.

"Yes," they replied.

Hyacinth ran upstairs to help Miss Josie and Mr. Jeet down the two flights to the ground floor. Mr. Jeet leaned heavily on Orlando, his grandnephew. Orlando was the same age as the twins, and he was strong from playing nearly every sport there was. He could probably have carried Mr. Jeet if necessary. After the kittens were sufficiently admired, Mama called everyone to the table, and Oliver breathed a sigh of relief. The carrots hadn't done a thing to assuage his hunger.

Oliver made his way to the dining room, where Papa was struggling to put in the extra table leaf. He helped push in the opposite sides of the table to nestle the extra piece in, and the twins pulled out the utensil drawer and sorted forks, spoons, and knives. Laney grabbed the napkins and laid them on the table, and Hyacinth set out trivets for the hot food.

"Oh, Orlando!" Mama said, catching sight of him. "I'm so glad you're here. I got you a pair of sneakers." She rummaged in the closet and came out with an impossibly huge box. "See if these fit you."

"Lucky," Oliver said, thinking about his own beat-up sneakers.

"I'm just waiting for sneakers your size to go on sale," Mama told Oliver.

Orlando didn't take the box. "Thank you, Mrs. Vanderbeeker, but it's too much. I can't accept them."

"Take them," Oliver said. "Mama probably got them on sale and then talked the manager into giving her an additional eighty percent off."

Mama shrugged. "What can I say? I excel at two things: bargaining and baking."

Oliver glanced at Orlando's sneakers, which he had left by the door. They were in a sorrier state than his own, which said a lot. Mama kept nudging the box toward him, and Orlando finally lifted the lid, took the shoes out, and slid his feet into them.

"Do they fit?" Mama asked.

"They're great," Orlando said. "Thanks, Mrs. Vanderbeeker."

"My pleasure," Mama said as she bustled into the kitchen to put out the final dishes.

Orlando took the shoes off and nestled them back in

the box in the tissue paper; then he pulled Jessie aside. "Hey, I forgot to tell you that my mom and I are taking off for a few days for spring break. I won't be around this week."

"Seriously?" Jessie said. "I thought we were going to work on our epic science fair project! I was thinking of a Rube Goldberg cat-feeding machine—"

"Yeah, sorry," Orlando interrupted. "We can work on it when I get back, right?"

"I guess," Jessie said. "This week would have been better, since we don't have school."

"Sorry," Orlando said again, not meeting her eyes.

"Dinner!" Mama called. "Grab a seat!"

People took their spots around the table, chatter and laughter filling the room. Mama passed platters across the kitchen island to Papa, who transferred them to the dining room table.

Miss Josie blessed the food, and when she had finished, Papa looked at Mama. "You've got a big birthday coming up. Any special requests?"

"When's your birthday?" Orlando asked.

"This Saturday," Mama said. "My one and only wish is to sleep in. My thirties were excellent but exhausting!" She picked up the platter of green beans and passed it around.

"Nothing could top your twenties, though," Papa said. "After all, that's when you met me." He flipped up the collar of his button-down work shirt and shot her his best grin.

"Oh jeez, Papa," Jessie and Isa said in unison.

"Young love," Miss Josie said to Mr. Jeet, squeezing his hand.

Mama smiled at Papa. "My twenties were pretty great, too."

"Come on, we're still waiting to hear what made your thirties so great," Uncle Arthur said.

"Well," Mama said, "I left my accountant job, for one thing. And I started my own baking business, which was the best career choice I have ever made."

The Vanderbeeker kids exchanged worried glances.

"It will forever be a mystery to me why you went into accounting," Uncle Arthur said. "Even when we were little, you were always fiddling around in the kitchen."

Mama shrugged. "I thought it would make our

parents happy. They wanted me to follow in Dad's footsteps."

"You shouldn't have listened to them," Uncle Arthur said.

"Hey," Mama said. "You should talk!" She glanced at the kids. "Guess what Uncle Arthur studied in college."

"They don't need to know," Uncle Arthur interjected, then turned to Oliver. "Hey, how about those treehouse plans, huh?"

"Ooh, a story about Uncle Arthur," Jessie said, rubbing her hands together.

"This is going to be good," Oliver said, taking a big bite of lasagna and waiting to be entertained.

Mama leaned in. "He wanted to study . . ." Mama gave a dramatic pause. ". . . exercise science."

"I don't even know what that is," murmured Miss Josie.

"I chose it because I liked sports," Uncle Arthur said. "The college catalogue was confusing."

"It's okay, honey," Auntie Harrigan said, patting his arm.

"How did you get into construction?" Orlando asked.

"I'd worked in construction every summer since high school, and halfway through college I was on summer break, working a construction job, and I realized I didn't care much about exercise science. So I pulled out of school and went into construction full-time." He looked at Mama and shrugged. "Our parents never forgave me."

"Why?" Oliver asked. "They didn't want you to have an awesome job?"

"They wanted me to be a doctor. Or a lawyer." Uncle Arthur grimaced. "Can you imagine me, a lawyer?"

"Nope," said Mama, Papa, Isa, Jessie, and Oliver.

"What about you, Papa?" Laney asked. "What did you want to do when you were little?"

"Oh, I've always wanted to work with computers," he said. "That's how I met your mother."

"We know," they all said at once.

They had heard the story of how Mama and Papa met dozens of times. Papa loved recounting how Mama had called the tech-help hotline at school when her computer showed the blank screen of death, and how Papa fell in love with her right away even though he hadn't laid eyes on her.

"Remember when you wanted to open your own bakery?" Papa asked Mama, then looked at their kids. "She dragged me all over the city to visit bakeries for research."

"That sounds awesome," Oliver said. Orlando and Mr. Jeet nodded in agreement.

"Did you have a name picked out?" Isa asked.

"Rainbow Sparkles Bakery," Laney declared. "That would be a good name."

Mama laughed, then glanced at Papa. "We came up with some good names, but I don't remember any of them. That was a long time ago, before any of you were born. Once Isa and Jessie arrived, there wasn't much time to think about it, so I started baking at home. That way I could still be with you all when you were little, but I could also earn money and do something I loved. It was a win-win-win situation."

Mama looked around the brownstone, her eyes lingering on the damaged walls

Oliver followed her eyes. "We should patch and paint, right?"

He watched his parents exchange glances. His mom cleared her throat.

"Maybe we can strategically place some framed pictures over the damaged areas," Mama said.

The doorbell rang, and Hyacinth and Laney raced for the door. Mr. Beiderman was back! Princess Cutie flew down the stairs and wrapped herself around his ankles, purring wildly. While everyone greeted him, Oliver saw Isa check her phone, her face brightening. She nudged Jessie and showed her the screen, and they did their wordless twin-conversation thing. Although Oliver couldn't understand their secret language, he knew one thing for certain: his sisters were up to something.

❋ ❋ ❋

After the Vanderbeeker kids were done cleaning up dinner, Isa called a family meeting. Usually when the Vanderbeekers had something on their minds, they would go up to the REP, the Roof of Epic Proportions, or to Jessie and Isa's room. But the day had been so rainy that the roof was one big puddle, and Jessie and Isa's room was also out because Hyacinth refused to go in there after an unfortunate incident in which she'd sat on one of Jessie's science experiments, a petri dish that was growing bacterial cultures swabbed from the bathroom sink.

Laney had deemed Oliver's bedroom the next official meeting place despite its being the smallest room in the entire brownstone. It had originally been a walk-in closet, so space was quite limited, but Oliver's younger sisters believed that only added to its charm. Hyacinth had sewn some floor pillows to go underneath the loft bed, and she and Laney had claimed that area as their own during family meetings. Jessie and Isa were relegated to sitting on the stacks of books in front of his overflowing bookcase, and Oliver sat on his desk chair. The kittens were set free once the door was closed and immediately beelined for Franz. They appeared to see him as a mother figure and loved cuddling up next to him and hiding under his ears.

"All right," Jessie said, *ahem*-ing loudly to get everyone's attention. "We need to figure out this animal dilemma. Hyacinth, you'll ask Mr. Beiderman if he

can take Franz, George Washington, and Paganini on Thursday, right?"

"I will, but doesn't that feel too much like lying?" said Hyacinth. "I mean, the inspector guy must have those rules for a purpose. People might have animal allergies. My friend Andrew is allergic to pistachios; he can't eat anything made in a kitchen that had pistachios in it. Will, Leah, and Kalyani are all allergic to peanuts."

"Well, what other ideas do you have?" Jessie asked. "We also have to figure out what to do with the kittens."

Hyacinth shrugged. "I don't have any other ideas, but this plan doesn't sound great to me."

Isa rubbed her eyes. "Maybe we should tell Mama about the whole thing. Come clean. Take the punishment."

"No way," Jessie objected. "Did you hear what Mama said about her business? How it's her dream job?"

"If we fail," Oliver said, "Mama will have found her dream job in her thirties and lost her dream job in her forties. And *Perch Magazine* will be a bust. Right before her birthday, too."

Isa's phone chimed, and she looked at the screen. She broke into a huge smile. "Hey, I have the best news, people!"

"Mama got her license back!" Laney said, jumping up and startling the kittens.

"Well, no," Isa said. "But this is second-best news. We can do something awesome to get the brownstone ready for the photo shoot. I got us free paint so we can paint the living room!"

"Paint! Paint! Paint!" Laney chanted.

"Shhh!" said all of her siblings.

"It's from Castleman's Bakery," Isa explained. "They bought the wrong color, and they couldn't return it."

"I can help, right?" Laney asked.

"We're all going to help," Isa said. "We are going to paint the whole downstairs."

Oliver narrowed his eyes. "You're not going to make Uncle Arthur use my treehouse time again, are you?"

"Nope," Isa said. "We're going to do this tonight, under the cover of darkness."

"Ooooh," said Oliver, Hyacinth, and Laney.

"It will be a surprise for Mama and Papa," Isa said. "When they wake up, ta-da! Brand-new paint job, all for free!"

"They're going to love it!" said Laney.

Isa smiled at her siblings. "Downstairs at midnight. Don't be late."

APRIL
MONDAY
1
TUESDAY
2
Find homes
for kittens!
WEDNESDA
3
S·P·R·I·N·G

Tuesday, April 2

HURSDAY	FRIDAY	SATURDAY
4	5	6
30p.m. Inspection	Perch Magazine Photo Shoot! Isa's Audition	Mama's Birthday!
B·R·E·A·K		

Twelve

It was time for Hyacinth and Laney to go to bed, but first the Vanderbeeker kids had to decide where the kittens would sleep. The argument got so heated that Mama stepped in to help negotiate. It was decided to keep the kittens in Laney and Hyacinth's room on one condition: they had to sleep in Franz's old dog crate. No amount of begging and pleading could convince Mama to let the kittens sleep on their beds, so Hyacinth lined the crate floor with towels that were soft with years of use and placed a shallow bin filled with kitty litter inside. Then she dragged her comforter and pillow down from the top bunk and set up a bed on the floor next to the crate. Laney made Isa and Jessie push the cage up against the edge of her bed so she was as close to the kittens as possible.

When Mama stepped out of the room to say goodbye to Uncle Arthur, Laney quickly found what she wanted to wear for bed: black leggings, black T-shirt, and black socks. She was ready to be a sneaky secret-agent painter at midnight. Then she jumped into bed and concealed her outfit underneath her covers.

When Mama returned to read the stack of books Laney had chosen for bedtime, her eyes narrowed in concern at Laney's bundled-up state. She pressed her hand to Laney's forehead. "Are you feeling okay?"

"Yes!" Laney blurted out. Then she said in a quieter voice, "Yes."

Mama took her hand away. "No fever."

"I feel great!" Laney said, wiggling with excitement. "I could stay up all night!"

Mama laughed. "Let's hope not." She glanced at the pile of picture books by the bed and raised an eyebrow. "All of these?"

Laney grinned. "Yes!"

Mama read all eight books, doing every voice perfectly and even throwing in some faces, and Laney's heart swelled with joy. She was so glad they were going to do something that was going to make Mama so happy. The brownstone would be the prettiest house the magazine people had ever seen, and she couldn't believe she was allowed to help with the actual painting! Uncle Arthur always told her that painting was a delicate job and that he would teach her when she got a little older, but maybe he had underestimated her abilities. She was going to be the best painter in all of history.

After the books, Mama gave Laney six good-night kisses, one for each year she had been alive. Then Mama knelt down by the kitten crate to say good night to Hyacinth. She gave Franz a scratch behind his ears before turning out the lights and closing the door. Laney lay in bed, wide awake. Mama was going to be so surprised when she woke up!

Hyacinth was less enthusiastic about trying to stay up until midnight; she really liked sleeping. Laney tried to keep Hyacinth awake by playing their favorite nighttime games, like drawing pictures on the wall with the beams of their flashlights and trying to guess what the images were. They also did a strobe-light extravaganza by clicking their flashlights off and on as quickly as possible. Pretty soon, though, Laney could tell Hyacinth was getting tired. She was in the middle of telling a very exciting story about the peregrine falcons that lived on the sides of tall buildings in New York City when Hyacinth began to snore.

Laney pulled off her covers, slipped out of bed, and crawled along the floor to where Franz was sleeping in his bed. He was also snoring. She lifted up his ear. "We've got a big mission today," she whispered, then proceeded to tell him all of her favorite foods for each letter of the alphabet.

Laney was on "mozzarella" for the letter "M" when the door creaked open and Jessie's face emerged from the darkness.

"You ready?" Jessie asked.

Laney jumped to her feet and ran to the door. "Ready!"

Jessie eyed her sister's clothing choices, then kneeled down to shake Hyacinth awake.

Hyacinth answered with a snore.

Jessie shook her again, and Hyacinth, who was used

to getting up in the middle of the night to accompany Laney to the bathroom, rubbed her eyes and followed her sisters out the door without protest.

The three sisters and Franz went downstairs as quietly as they could. Laney could hear the white-noise machine whirring in Mama and Papa's bedroom. When she was a baby, the machine had belonged to her. After a couple of years, she didn't need it anymore, and Mama tried it out herself to see if it would help her sleep better. It worked, so she kept it.

Hyacinth was the expert at navigating the stairs as soundlessly as possible, so she went down first, and Jessie and Laney followed in her exact footsteps. Oliver and Isa were already downstairs, and Isa was bringing paint cans inside from where Benny had left them on their doorstep a couple of hours earlier.

Oliver was using blue painter's tape to line the baseboards, entryways, and windows. Tarps and bedsheets covered the floor. Laney knew Oliver was an expert at painting because he had helped Uncle Arthur paint his apartment once. She hoped they could use those stilt things to reach high-up places.

"Are we ready?" Isa said. She waved a paintbrush in the air like a warrior's declaration. "This is going to be awesome. Mama is going to be so happy!"

While Jessie patched the damaged walls with joint compound, Oliver pried a can open with a screwdriver, then stirred the paint with a wooden stick. "Are we really painting the walls this color?"

Laney peered into the can. The paint was a beautiful rose pink, the same color as her favorite socks. "Oooh, this is pretty."

"Isn't it?" Isa said. Then she looked at the scuffed white walls. "I think this will be perfect for this room."

Oliver's professional opinion was that they should begin on the west wall, since it wasn't covered with bookcases. Laney grabbed a brush and dipped it into the paint, and to her surprise no one tried to stop her. This was shaping up to be the absolute best night in history!

* * *

Two hours later, the excitement over being awake way past their bedtime had lost its sheen. The brownstone did not murmur, creak, or whistle, and the quiet extended beyond their apartment. The dogs of 141st Street were all asleep, the ambulance sirens were silent, and the streets were empty of cars. Jessie was not used to hearing nothing. For some reason, the silence seemed very, very loud.

Jessie put down her brush after working on a particularly challenging corner, which had caused her to turn her neck in an unpleasant way, and now she put her brush down and rolled her head to loosen all the stiff muscles. Next to her, Laney was lying on the ground, her brush hanging loosely from her hand as she ran the bristles against the same area over and over again, getting most of the paint on the blue tape or the tarp.

Oliver was standing on a chair, trying to reach up high with his paint roller. Hyacinth had given up half an hour earlier and was asleep on the couch with Franz as a pillow. Isa was the most productive of them all; she was painting feverishly with the other roller, with no sign of slowing down.

Jessie looked at her sister, wondering where this burst of productivity had come from. "Everything okay?" Jessie asked.

"Of course," Isa said.

Jessie put her brush down and stared at her sister. "Is something bothering you?"

Isa's answer was quick—too quick. "Nope."

Jessie dipped her brush back into the paint. "Okay."

They continued to paint in silence. Of course Jessie knew what was bothering Isa. It was the audition, it was Mama's business, it was all those things Isa could not control. But Jessie knew Isa could handle it all and more. She wanted to tell her that, to really make her sister trust that it was true, but she knew it was one of those things Isa needed to figure out on her own.

An hour later, Oliver had fallen asleep on the couch, and Laney was snoozing on the tarp with her paint-brush still in her hand. Even Isa was fading. Jessie was sitting in an armchair, struggling to stay awake to keep Isa company, when she saw Isa put her paintbrush down and collapse into the armchair next to hers.

"I'm just resting my eyes for a second," she told Jessie. Then they both promptly fell asleep.

A few minutes later, Paganini, curious about what Laney had been doing all night, hopped into the middle of the living room. He stood on his hind legs to peer into the paint can. Then he rested his front two paws on top of the can and tipped it over. Paint oozed over the can lip.

No one saw the pink paint spread out on the tarp in the shape of Antarctica. No one saw it pool in Laney's hair as she slept.

No one saw Paganini hop into the spilled paint, then kick and jump frantically around the living room to get it off his feet.

Instead, the Vanderbeekers slept and the brownstone slept. Paganini, having by now sufficiently stamped enough of the pink paint off his paws, hunkered down in the corner by the new bookshelves and kept watch over the night.

Thirteen

The sun came up and touched Harlem that morning, revealing a deep blue sky without a trace of clouds. Hyacinth woke to find herself on the couch, Franz tucked in right next to her. His tail waved a good morning when she met his eyes.

Sunshine glittered through the large living room windows, and Hyacinth looked outside and noticed that everything was bright and clean, her absolute favorite kind of day to wake up to. After a good, solid rain, Harlem always looked brand-new, as if someone had run it through a vigorous car wash. Beautiful, shiny days always made her feel like the hours before her were full of possibilities, which was a good thing because it seemed important to hope this week.

Ready to begin the day, Hyacinth sat up so she faced the center of the brownstone. But at the sight of the living room, she blinked, rubbed her eyes, then looked again.

The paint, which had looked like a romantic rose color in the darkness of the previous night, was so blindingly bright in the early-morning light that Hyacinth winced. It was as if a cotton-candy machine had exploded. Even worse, pink rabbit-sized paw-prints dotted the floor, carpet, and the seat of their favorite yellow reading chair. Hyacinth's eyes frantically scanned the room for Paganini. She located him in the corner next to a potted plant. He was staring at her with an "It wasn't me!" face despite the pink paint stuck to the fur around his feet and at the tips of his long whiskers.

Hyacinth tried to get off the couch, but she got tangled in Franz's limbs and the blanket and tumbled to the ground with a yelp.

Jessie bolted up from her sleeping spot in the purple armchair. "Don't let the petri dishes break!" she yelled.

Isa groaned and draped an arm over her eyes. "Ow. My arm muscles are sore from painting all night."

Franz trotted over to Oliver and licked his face.

"Yick," Oliver said, rubbing the slobber off.

Laney was the last to open her eyes. "Is it time to get up?"

"Holy smokes!" Jessie exclaimed, jumping out of the armchair and pointing at the stiff pink paint globs in Laney's hair. "What happened to you?"

Laney's eyes widened. "What?"

All five Vanderbeekers were suddenly completely awake, and they quickly saw that Laney's hair was the least of their worries.

"Oh my gosh, that paint is *nuts*," Isa muttered, looking at the wall. "How did this happen? The color is giving me a headache."

"Maybe because we painted with only one light on," Oliver suggested.

"Paint is on the reading chair!" Laney yelled. "Someone is in serious trouble!"

"Paganini," Hyacinth said simply, pointing at the culprit. Paganini stretched out his front legs and gave a big yawn; then he settled back into a ball and closed his eyes.

"Oh my gosh, Mama is going to kill us," Jessie moaned.

"Why is Mama going to kill you?" Papa called as he descended the staircase.

The Vanderbeekers froze.

Papa got to the bottom of the stairs, and his head swiveled to take in the scene. His mouth fell open. The Vanderbeeker kids didn't dare breathe.

"You're absolutely right," Papa said at last. "Mama is going to flip."

"We can explain everything," Jessie said.

"My hair feels weird," Laney said.

Papa sighed. "You guys are in big trouble."

"Our intentions were honorable," Isa told him.

"You can explain later while we're cleaning up," Papa said. "First, let's try to fix this before Mama sees it."

* * *

Jessie watched Isa carry Paganini into the bathroom, his legs kicking out furiously as he tried to escape. Isa had assigned herself the immense job of bathing Laney and Paganini as penance for coming up with the terrible paint idea, and Hyacinth was tasked with feeding the kittens and cleaning their litterbox.

After the bathroom door closed, locking Isa inside with Paganini and Laney, Jessie googled "how to remove paint from hardwood floor." Google instructed them to use a plastic putty knife to scrape the not-quite-dry latex paint off the wood. Oliver ran to borrow supplies from Mr. Smiley, the superintendent of the big building two doors down and the father of his best friend, Angie. He had an impressive storehouse of tools in the building's basement.

Jessie was blotting the carpet (*not* scrubbing—Google specifically said *not* to scrub) with paper towels when Oliver returned. Papa was unzipping the yellow couch cover while interrogating his daughters about the paint situation.

"We wanted to help beautify the brownstone for the photo shoot," Jessie explained. "We know you've been wanting to paint the living room, and Benny had paint they weren't using from when the Castlemans repainted the store."

Papa raised one eyebrow. "I don't remember their bakery being painted this color."

"That's because they decided to go with Saguaro Blossom Yellow instead," Hyacinth explained as she came down the stairs, finished with attending to the kittens. She joined Jessie at the carpet.

"Smart," Papa said, laying the couch covering on the floor and blotting away. He had a cup with water and dish detergent to help.

Oliver took a putty knife and got to work scraping the paint from the floor.

"Next time, please obtain the proper parental consent before painting our apartment fuchsia," Papa said. *Blot, blot, blot.* "Ugh, it's so tempting to scrub."

"We thought we were helping," Jessie said. "Don't worry, we'll fix it before the photo shoot."

"I want white paint this time," Papa said. "Good old boring white paint, please."

"Yes, Papa," the kids said.

"We probably need five coats of primer to make sure the pink doesn't show through," Oliver grumbled. *Scrape, scrape, scrape.*

Jessie had a thought: maybe fuchsia was one of those colors that look unexpectedly wonderful on camera. She pulled her phone from her back pocket and snapped a photo to test her theory. She looked at the image. The wall glowed and turned all the objects around it pink.

Nope, they definitely couldn't keep the wall fuchsia.

* * *

When Mama got up, Papa intercepted her as she came down the stairs and handed her a cup of coffee and the newspaper. Then he told her to get back to bed and that he'd let her know when it was safe to come out again.

Mama made the mistake of glancing around. "What in the world—"

"Trust me," Papa said. He put his hands on her shoulders and swiveled her back toward the bedroom. "It's better not to know."

It took nearly two hours to clean the floors, the carpet, the couch, Laney, and Paganini. Isa used one and a half bottles of shampoo to gently comb through the paint-covered strands of hair. Laney emerged from the bathroom grumpy and with a sore scalp from all the pulling, and Paganini was similarly disgruntled (but remarkably fluffy) after his bath and the subsequent blow-dry to keep him from getting a chill.

Oliver was able to get most of the paint off the floor by using the plastic putty knife, but the carpets and armchair cover did not fare so well: even after all the blotting, they still had large spots of pinkish hues. Everyone crossed their fingers that the color would fade once everything had dried.

It was at that point that Papa brought Mama downstairs to examine the fuchsia paint job.

The Vanderbeekers gathered around and waited for the verdict.

"It's terrible," Mama finally said. "We can't keep it like this." She exchanged glances with Papa, then murmured, "I think we need to dip into the Fiver Account."

"Not the Fiver Account!" Papa whispered in horror.

"What's the Fiver Account?" Laney asked. She had really good ears.

Mama and Papa looked at each other for a long moment; then Mama finally said, "For the past two years, we've been putting any five-dollar bills we get into a can we nailed into the corner of our bedroom closet. It was a bizarre idea we had one night."

The Vanderbeeker kids were speechless. Apparently there were things their parents did that they had no idea about. Even Laney, who had a gift for snooping, didn't know about the can.

"I got the idea from a book I loved when I was a teenager," Mama said. "It was called *A Tree Grows in Brooklyn,* and in the story, the mom saves extra pennies and nickels and puts them in a can in the closet."

"Like a savings account?" Jessie said.

"Sort of," Papa said. "We already have a separate savings account, so this is like . . . fun money. We were hoping we could save enough to go on a family trip one day."

The Vanderbeeker kids burst into chatter.

"That's so cool!" Hyacinth said. "Could we go to Monterey Bay Aquarium?" Hyacinth had wanted to visit that aquarium since she was five years old.

"I think we should go to Europe," Isa said. "There are so many great concert halls there. Bach lived there. Mozart lived there!"

Before the other kids could chime in with their

dream vacations, Mama held up a hand. "I definitely want to hear all of your ideas, and I hope one day we'll be able to take a big trip together. But right now, I think we need to dive into the Fiver Account for paint. I'll ask Uncle Arthur whether he gets a discount at the hardware store." At her kids' distraught faces, she added, "We'll save up again. One day, we'll have enough."

The kids looked at one another. They couldn't think of a more terrible way to use the Fiver Account than buying boring white paint.

Mama sank down onto the couch and rolled her shoulders.

Hyacinth, who was by the back door ready to let Franz out, yelped. "There are guinea pigs outside!"

Fourteen

Laney knew just what to do with guinea pigs—her kindergarten classroom had two as pets, and she had taken care of them all winter break, so she considered herself a professional. She marched right up to the back door and opened it. In a box with the top open sat two guinea pigs on a bed of hay. They were chewing contentedly.

One of the guinea pigs was brown and white, with hair that looked like Papa's and Oliver's when they woke up in the morning. The other had short hair the color of a lion.

Behind Laney stood the rest of her family. They wore a mixture of expressions, from astonished

(Hyacinth and Oliver) to concerned (Isa and Jessie), amused (Papa), and resigned (Mama).

"Where are these animals coming from?" Isa exclaimed.

"This is nuts," Oliver said.

"Don't worry," Laney announced, picking up the box and bringing it inside. "I am a Guinea Pig Expert. I will take care of them."

"Aren't guinea pigs a type of rodent?" Mama asked with a shudder.

"Yes, they are," answered Laney, Guinea Pig Expert. "So are beavers, prairie dogs, chipmunks, and capybaras."

"Really?" Papa said.

"Rodents account for forty percent of all mammal species," Jessie chimed in. "They are found in huge numbers on every continent except Antarctica."

"Is there a guinea pig rescue organization?" Isa asked. "We can't keep them here."

"But they're so cute!" Laney said. "Look at their noses!"

Isa ignored Laney. "We have to find out who's

leaving these animals. Yesterday it was kittens; today it's guinea pigs."

"Maybe tomorrow it will be pigs," Hyacinth said hopefully. "Pigs are really smart. I've always wanted one."

Mama and Papa looked at each other. Then Papa said, "Your mom and I have busy days, so you're on your own with this one. We've got to get ready for work."

"Just leave the tarps where they are." Mama gestured toward one fuchsia wall. "We'll need them when we repaint. Isa, Jessie, and Oliver, you're in charge of cleaning all the brushes. Laney and Hyacinth, you are forbidden to touch paint again until you're old enough to vote. And, Laney, under no circumstances are you to let the guinea pigs out of that box!"

"Yes, Mama," they chorused, and Mama and Papa went upstairs to shower and change while Laney ransacked the refrigerator for vegetables suitable for guinea pigs. Oliver ran across the street to borrow Angie's cage—her guinea pig Phee-Phee had died the winter before—and when he returned, Laney got to work. She dusted off the cage, lined the bottom with newspaper, filled the water bottle, put some of Paganini's hay into the hay rack, and cut up leafy greens. Then she carefully transported the guinea pigs to their new habitat and watched as they instantly went for the vegetables.

The latch secured, Laney put the cage on the dining room table, and the Vanderbeekers sat around it and stared at the guinea pigs. The kittens were frolicking at their feet, Franz was doing laps around the table, George Washington was glaring at the kittens from his perch on the windowsill, and Paganini was chewing a giant hole in the abandoned cardboard box the guinea pigs had been delivered in.

Isa crossed her arms and rested her chin on her hands. "This situation is getting out of control. How are we going to get all these animals out of here *and* remove all evidence of them by Thursday morning? That's two days away."

Laney stood up. "Hyacinth and I are going to see Mr. Beiderman. He knows all sorts of things. Maybe he knows who's leaving them at our door."

"Don't forget to ask him about keeping the animals in his apartment during the inspection," Oliver said.

Laney nodded, then looked around for any cookies Mama might have left behind from her orders. Sometimes Mr. Beiderman was in a bad mood, and when they wanted a favor, they knew it was best to arrive prepared.

* * *

Hyacinth and Laney picked out the most perfect cookies from the ones Mama had left and put them in a Tupperware container. Laney grabbed the guinea pig cage, and together they went upstairs to introduce the new animals to Mr. Beiderman.

"Who is it?" boomed Mr. Beiderman at Hyacinth's knock on the door.

"It sounds like he's in a bad mood," Laney whispered to Hyacinth.

"Good thing we brought cookies," Hyacinth replied.

"I heard that," Mr. Beiderman said as he opened the door.

"Heard what?" Hyacinth said, her eyes wide and innocent.

Mr. Beiderman grunted. "What kind of cookies did you bring? Wait, what are those? Rodents?"

“That’s right!” Laney said.

He tried to close the door on them. “I don’t want rodents in my apartment.”

“They’re guinea pigs,” Laney clarified as she pushed her way inside. “They’re *cute* rodents.”

Princess Cutie leaped down from the top of her three-tiered deluxe cat tree, where she had been napping, and sauntered toward the cage. She stared at the guinea pigs, then backed away, her tail sticking straight up as if she had been electrocuted.

“Don’t tell me you got *more* animals,” Mr. Beiderman said. “Weren’t the kittens enough?”

“We found these this morning,” Laney told him.

“They were left in a box outside our door,” Hyacinth explained. “Have you seen anyone suspicious leaving animals at people’s doorsteps?”

“No,” Mr. Beiderman said. “But I just got home last night.”

“You should adopt the guinea pigs or one of the kittens,” Hyacinth said. “I think Princess Cutie would like a friend.”

Princess Cutie hissed and swatted a paw at the guinea pigs’ cage. Mr. Beiderman scooped her up, and she immediately began to purr in his arms. "I think Princess Cutie likes getting *all* the attention. And I don't want rodents in my apartment."

"What about one of the kittens?" Hyacinth suggested. "I can run downstairs and bring them up so you can look at them again."

Princess Cutie was peering over Mr. Beiderman's shoulder, her cat eyes narrowed to slits as she stared at the guinea pigs.

"No," Mr. Beiderman said firmly. "This is a one-cat household."

Laney looked up at him with her Super Sad Puppy Eyes, but Mr. Beiderman was immune to her charms.

"Okay, fine," Hyacinth said, "but would you be willing to take Franz, Paganini, and George Washington on Thursday for a couple of hours?"

"No, thank you," Mr. Beiderman said. Princess Cutie purred in agreement.

"But Mr. Beiderman!" Hyacinth protested. "We just took care of Princess Cutie for five whole days while you were at your conference!"

"Princess Cutie is a polite, well-mannered cat. You're asking me to look after three wild animals!"

"They aren't wild!" Laney said.

"Last time Franz was in my apartment, he ate four dish towels," Mr. Beiderman pointed out.

"He was hungry," Hyacinth explained. "He had just started his diet."

"And Paganini dug a huge hole in the pot of my ficus," Mr. Beiderman added. "He scratched up all the roots and killed the tree."

"We bought a new one for you," Hyacinth reminded him.

"I liked my old tree," Mr. Beiderman grumbled. "And don't forget George Washington threw up on my couch *and* on my bed."

"We're very sorry about that," Hyacinth said. "The change of environment stressed him out."

"You should help us," Laney declared. "Did you know that Princess Cutie woke us all up at five in the morning every day? She's super loud when she's hungry."

Mr. Beiderman shut his eyes and took a deep breath. "Fine. Your pets can come over for two hours, max. Bring a leash for Franz. Leave Paganini in his carrier. Why do you need them out of the apartment?"

"There's an inspection," Hyacinth said. She didn't mention that it was a kitchen inspection, and it felt a bit icky to fudge the truth that way. *It's just a temporary fix,* Hyacinth said to herself. *Only until the photo shoot is done.*

Mr. Beiderman nodded, trusting that he wasn't being pulled into a nefarious plot. "Fine, fine."

Hyacinth gave him a wobbly smile, and Laney began telling Mr. Beiderman all her ideas for guinea pig names while Hyacinth chewed on her lip and worried about whether she had just told a lie.

Fifteen

Jessie was tired. Between being awake most of the night and cleaning up the paint disaster, she felt completely beat. She didn't understand how Isa could already be downstairs practicing after the night they had.

The kittens had a lot more energy than she did. She watched them scramble over one another in the pen Hyacinth had cobbled together, using a combination of boxes and stacks of books. Franz, who had gotten very attached to the kittens, hung his head over the top of the pen and whimpered until Hyacinth let him inside.

Biting into a warm blueberry muffin, Jessie turned her attention to the kitchen, where Mama was packing up her orders for the day. Oliver gave her an uneasy glance. They really hoped Mr. West didn't find out that Mama was operating her business without a license. A brief image of Mama behind bars, wearing an orange jumpsuit, flashed through Jessie's head but was interrupted when a clumping sound revealed Papa giving Laney a piggyback ride down the stairs, Hyacinth following with the guinea pig cage in her arms. Papa had changed out of his coveralls and was wearing his "computer work clothes": pants with a collared button-down.

"You will not believe the work request I just received," he told them. He was remarkably cheerful, given the unexpected three-hour paint-clean-up job that had caused him to be late for work. Laney refused to let go when he tried to drop of her off at a stool, so Papa made his way to Mama, and they both gave her a kiss on the cheek.

"What's your work request?" Oliver asked.

"I get to see if I can restore an IBM computer from 1992," Papa said, a smile taking over his face. "MS-DOS, baby!"

"That doesn't sound fun," Oliver said around a mouthful of muffin.

"What's MS-DOS?" Isa said, coming up from the basement.

"Now you've done it," Oliver muttered.

"Oh, it's brilliant!" Papa said, grabbing a muffin. "It's a nongraphic command-line operating system derived from 86-DOS. So instead of using a mouse or a keypad to navigate Microsoft Windows, you can use command lines. Isn't that awesome?"

"So awesome," the kids murmured.

Mama glanced at Papa and smiled, then turned away to put a dish in the sink. Isa opened the refrigerator door and picked up a glass jar filled with a smoothie she had made the night before. Jessie watched Oliver snatch a muffin when Mama's back was turned—he had finished the first one moments after he grabbed it—and go back to sit on his stool, but Isa had beaten him to it. He was forced to take the seat Laney usually sat in, the least desirable one, due to his youngest sister's tendency to eat with her hands and then wipe her fingers along the edge of the counter.

"At least it's not another phone dropped in the toilet," Papa continued. "Did you know that's considered a biohazard? We have to use gloves. Safety first."

"Ick," Laney said, still hanging on to him, fiddling with the ID tag clipped to the pocket of his shirt.

"What are you up to today?" Papa asked the kids.

"Uncle Arthur is coming to work on the treehouse," Oliver said.

"I need to practice for my audition," Isa said.

"I'm going to help Allegra make kitten flyers," Laney said.

"And then we're going to post them all around the neighborhood," Jessie added.

"I'm going to knit house slippers for Franz," Hyacinth said.

"That sounds like a great—" Papa began, then looked at Hyacinth. "Wait, what did you say?"

"I'm going to knit house slippers for Franz," Hyacinth repeated. "His feet get cold."

They all turned to look at Franz. He was sprawled out among the kittens, belly up and ears flipped open.

"How would he keep them on?" Oliver wondered aloud.

"Velcro," Hyacinth explained.

"I'm sure he'll be very appreciative," Mama said as she made her way to the door with her bakery boxes. "When is Uncle Arthur coming?"

"In a couple of hours," Oliver said.

"Don't forget to ask him about the paint! We need to get that wall fixed before the photo shoot," Mama said before disappearing out the door.

Jessie felt her stomach squeeze. The thought of having to repaint the fuchsia wall—and using the Fiver Account to do it—made the muffin she had just eaten sit like a rock in her stomach.

❊ ❊ ❊

Allegra sent Isa a text saying she would come by later that morning, so Isa decided to practice in the basement until her friend arrived. She tackled a particularly challenging section of her audition piece over and over again, until she finally put her violin down and rolled her head to release some of the tension that had built up in her neck and shoulders. The passage was filled with double stops, places where she had to play two strings at once, and spiccato bow strokes, where the bow had to bounce on the string like a stone skipping on water.

She was just about to pick up her violin again when the doorbell rang. Isa nestled the violin in its case and jogged up the steps and across the living room, then looked through the peephole. There was Allegra. She had a drawing pad under one arm and a handful of dresses covered in plastic draped over her other arm.

"Are we ready for dress fittings?" Allegra asked when Isa opened the door.

"Um," Isa said, "I thought we were going to make flyers."

"I'm multitasking," Allegra said. "Hey, where is everyone?"

"I'm not sure," Isa said, "but don't question it. I'm enjoying the quiet."

Allegra squeezed past Isa and kicked off her shoes in the entryway. When she reached the living room, she froze, and the drawing pad and dresses fell to the ground. "What the heck happened in here?" she said, staring at the fuchsia wall.

"It looked like a rose color in the dark," Isa explained. "We're going to paint over it."

"Paint *over* it?" Allegra said. "Why? This color is *gorgeous!*"

"Really?" Isa stood next to her, and they both stared at the wall.

"I'm in love with it," Allegra said. "It's perfect. I say keep it."

Isa had to look away. The color was too much. "We have to repaint. It's not going to work for the photo shoot."

Allegra tilted her head. "I guess you're right. Wow, I want my whole bedroom to be this color."

"Seriously?" Isa said. She pointed to the leftover paint cans. "If you want, take them."

Allegra squealed. "Oh my gosh! My parents are going to flip!"

Isa helped Allegra pick up her drawing pad and the dresses. "So what are these?"

"Outfits for your audition, of course," Allegra said. "Dress for success and all that."

"I was going to wear my recital clothes for the audition," Isa said.

Allegra clutched her chest. "Your *recital* clothes? Girl, don't give me a heart attack. You are *not* wearing those drab black pants and that white button-down! As your best friend, I cannot stand by and watch you do that to yourself. Now, which one do you like best?" She picked up the first one from the pile. It was a glittery, floor-length gold dress. "What do you think?"

Isa gave a strangled "No."

Allegra held the dress toward Isa and squinted. "You're right. This is too Oscar-ish. We'll save it for when you solo at Carnegie Hall." She tossed it to the side and picked up a yellow one. "How about this?" She didn't even let Isa answer before she tossed that one aside too. "That color won't look good on you. Ooh, what about this one? Hold it up in front of you."

Isa obeyed, and Allegra nodded.

"Yup, this is the one," Isa agreed. It was a black dress with lace details at the collar and sleeves, and Isa thought it said "elegant and professional," exactly the combination she was looking for.

"Try it on," Allegra said, settling down on the couch with her sketchpad. "And be quick. I'm hungry."

Isa dutifully took the dress to the downstairs bathroom. As she put it on, she heard Allegra talking to their rabbit.

"Paganini, you are just too cute," Allegra crooned. "I know you want to come home with me. I can sneak you out in my jacket and you can be the rabbit king of my apartment."

Isa smiled as she zipped up the dress and went back into the living room. She spread her arms out. "What do you think?"

"Spin," Allegra commanded, twirling a finger.

Isa did a 360, and Allegra nodded with satisfaction. "My duty as best friend is done. You look perfect. Now let's find your siblings and get to work on those kitten flyers."

Sixteen

Isa and Allegra found Hyacinth and Laney asleep on their bedroom floor next to the guinea pig cage. The kittens were batting at Hyacinth's braids.

Allegra narrowed her eyes at the cage and whispered, "Guinea pigs? Really?"

Isa shook her head. "Don't ask."

They gently woke Hyacinth and Laney, then got Oliver, who was reading in bed, and Jessie, who was hunched over a notebook in her room. Together they went downstairs with the guinea pigs and the kittens and worked on the flyers.

"Can you draw guinea pigs?" Jessie asked Allegra.

Laney glared at Jessie. "Why are you asking that?"

"We can't keep the guinea pigs!" Jessie said.

"But I'm a Guinea Pig Expert," Laney said, her hands on her hips. "I'll take care of them."

Isa pulled Laney into her lap. "I know this is hard. I wish we could keep all these animals too."

The low rumble of a truck engine indicating Uncle Arthur's arrival provided a welcome distraction, and Oliver raced outside to help his uncle bring in tools. Uncle Arthur froze when he walked in the door and saw the bright fuchsia walls in the living room, as well as the tarps covering the ground. "What the . . ."

"The color looked different in the nighttime," Oliver said.

"It couldn't have looked *that* different," Uncle Arthur responded.

"I think it's fantastic," Allegra said. "I'm going to paint my bedroom that color."

"How much would it cost to fix it and repaint it white?" Isa asked.

Uncle Arthur stared at the wall, then looked away and blinked really hard. "Wow, that color is making me dizzy. Okay, if you want to repaint it—and I think you definitely should—you need to use a high-hide primer. It's specially made to cover dark colors. Two coats will do the trick. I've got some left over from when we painted our apartment. Remember when we first moved in and the previous tenant had painted his bedroom all black? The high-hide primer worked great on that room. That way you would just need to buy two cans of the paint color you want. Hopefully the next color you choose will be less . . . uh, vibrant."

"Can you bring the primer tomorrow?" Oliver said. "The living room needs to be perfect by Friday."

"Sure," Uncle Arthur said. "Get the paint today, and we can fix the wall tomorrow."

The Vanderbeekers breathed a sigh of relief.

"We owe you bigtime," Isa said.

Uncle Arthur grinned. "Be sure to remember how amazing I am when Christmas comes." Then his smile disappeared. "What is *that?*" he asked, pointing at the guinea pig cage.

"Guinea pigs," Laney told him.

Uncle Arthur sighed. "You know what? I'm not even going to ask."

❋ ❋ ❋

The kitten and guinea pig flyers done, Allegra said goodbye, and Jessie, Hyacinth, and Laney went back to the library, this time to use the photocopier. Oliver stayed behind to supervise all the pets and work on his treehouse with Uncle Arthur, and Isa went back down to the basement to practice.

As they made their way through Harlem, Hyacinth kept her eyes peeled for bulbs pushing up through the soil in the tree pits along the sidewalk. Hyacinth loved flower bulbs, probably because she was named after one. Her favorites (beside hyacinths) were daffodils, and those were out in abundance that morning. To Hyacinth, the yellow against the gray sidewalks was the most beautiful color combination in the world.

The library was brick, with swirling iron work in front of all the windows. A brass plaque attached to the front entry announced that it had been built back in 1891. Jessie pushed open the heavy wooden doors, and they stepped inside. Hyacinth breathed in the smell of books and let the hushed voices wrap around her.

The Vanderbeekers waved to the librarians at the ground-floor circulation desk, then made their way upstairs to the children's section on the second floor. Hyacinth tried to put her feet in the exact middle of the marble grooves of the steps. She liked thinking that she was walking in the footsteps made by thousands of people going up and down these same stairs over the last one hundred years.

When they got upstairs, they went in search of Ms. Abruzzi, the nicest and most fashionable children's librarian in all of Harlem. They found her sitting on the floor next to the picture book stacks, reading one of Hyacinth's personal favorites, *Bee-bim Bop!,* out loud to a handful of enraptured four-year-olds. Ms. Abruzzi wore black combat boots, a green dress printed with hundreds of colorful butterflies, and long silver earrings with tiny pink dinosaurs hanging from the ends of the chains.

After she was done reading, she looked up and saw the Vanderbeekers.

"Back so soon! How are the kittens?" she asked.

"Great," Jessie told her; then she handed over the flyers. "We also have guinea pigs. Can you help us? We need to make copies of these adoption flyers."

"Sure," she said. Her black combat boots clomped along the floor as she led them to the copier machine. She ran off twenty-five copies each of the kitten and guinea pig flyers, then refused to let them pay for it because "finding homes for abandoned pets is the epitome of good deeds and love." Hyacinth gave her a hug, then memorized Ms. Abruzzi's outfit so she could replicate it one day.

The Vanderbeekers hung flyers in the library, one of each by the two circulating desks; then they headed outside and taped them to lampposts and in the windows of Castleman's Bakery, Harlem Coffee, A to Z Deli, and Hiba's Hardware Store. While they were at Hiba's, they picked up two cans of the most boring eggshell-white paint they could find. Fortunately, Hiba gave them a discount and the paint was affordable enough that they could pay for it from their shared allowances. They breathed a sigh of relief. Sure, they'd messed up bigtime, possibly destroyed Mama's dream, and were now broke, but at least the Fiver Account remained untouched.

❂ ❂ ❂

Before they got to work on the treehouse, Oliver and Uncle Arthur made a quick stop in the kitchen to snag a couple of muffins and had a brief debate about the superiority of muffins versus cookies (Uncle Arthur was Team Muffin, which Oliver could not understand). Then they went outside and put together their game plan.

"This is going to be easy," Uncle Arthur said. "We've already got the platform, plus we've framed the walls.

All we have to do now is put on the siding, install the walls, and add the roof."

"Since this project is so easy, can we do two floors?" Oliver asked. "I have the plans already drawn up."

Uncle Arthur laughed, then said, "We'll see," which Oliver took as a yes.

"Have you ever made a treehouse before?" Oliver asked as they set up their work site.

"Sure I have. Didn't I tell you the story of when your mom and I put a treehouse in Ottenville Park?" he asked. Ottenville was where Mama and Uncle Arthur had grown up. Oliver's grandparents still lived there.

"Really?" Oliver said as he pounded a nail into the treehouse frame. "Whose idea was that?"

"Your mom's," Uncle Arthur said. "And she forced me to help her. Back then, your mom was pretty annoying once she got an idea in her head." He paused. "Actually, she's still sort of like that now."

"Why didn't you build one in your backyard?" Oliver asked.

"We lived in a little apartment," Uncle Arthur said. "Your grandparents didn't move into their house until after we all finished college. Anyway, your mom had this idea that she was going to start a baking business and she would run the shop out of the treehouse. She said I could share in half the profits if I built the treehouse for her, so I agreed."

"How old were you?" Oliver asked.

"Oh, we were in middle school. A little older than you are now. Back then we had to take wood shop in school, and my best friend's dad was in construction. He thought the treehouse was a great hands-on learning experience, so we collected materials and he helped us put it up. We were even able to pass it off as a final project for the class. When it was done, your mom painted it bright pink and white and put streamers and a sign on it. Summer had just started, so she figured she could spend all her time baking and selling cookies and brownies from the treehouse. We designed a pulley so she could collect money in exchange for baked goods. It went great for about six days."

"Then what happened?" Oliver asked.

"The Parks Department found out about it and

MAIA'S
BAKERY
Cookie Delivery System

made your mom stop. Said it was illegal to operate a business without a license."

"That doesn't make sense!" Oliver said. "Kids sell lemonade and Girl Scout cookies all the time."

"Selling the baked goods was illegal, and apparently putting up a treehouse on government property was also illegal, so we had to take down the treehouse, too."

"After all that work?"

"Yes," Uncle Arthur said. "Hey, help me with this siding." They attached the side wall to a pulley he had strung high in a tree, and they pulled it up until it rested on the platform. They repeated the work for the other sides, and then it was time to install them.

There wasn't much talking after that, because power tools make a lot of noise; plus sawdust was flying around, and Oliver didn't want to get any in his mouth. But as they worked, he thought about Uncle Arthur and Mama doing this same thing decades earlier. For some reason, Oliver never thought about Mama as a kid. He certainly never knew she had started a treehouse bakery.

Uncle Arthur was like a machine, and pretty soon

all four walls were in place. They continued to work the rest of the day, pausing only for lunch, and by dinner the siding was up and secured, and a small second story had been added.

Oliver was sore, sweaty, and covered in sawdust. He couldn't remember a better day.

Seventeen

Papa came home that night energized from his MS-DOS victory, skidding to a stop when he reached the living room. Franz and the five kittens scrambled to greet him and careened into his feet.

Papa sniffed the air. "Is it taco night?"

Taco night was a once-a-month tradition, and Papa and Laney in particular loved tacos with the force of a thousand suns. Since Uncle Arthur had been working on the treehouse all afternoon, he joined them (he also loved tacos). After Mama said grace, everyone dug into the food.

Laney was careful to load up her taco shell to optimize the amount of diced tomatoes she could fit inside. This required a delicate balance of creating little pockets in the meat, lettuce, and cheese so the tomatoes could nestle inside without danger of falling out.

"We made good progress today," Uncle Arthur said. "I think we can finish the treehouse tomorrow."

Oliver, who had been cramming tacos into his mouth at a remarkable rate, raised his free hand into the air in victory.

Laney paused in her tomato placement to look at Oliver. "So does that mean I can have your room?"

Oliver froze mid-bite. "Why would you get my room?" he finally asked around a mouthful of food.

"Oliver, manners," Mama scolded.

Laney pointed her taco at him. "Because you're moving into the treehouse."

Oliver's face turned stormy as he swallowed. "I'm not moving into the treehouse! Why would you think that?"

Laney's eyebrows shot in toward each other. "But that's not fair that you get a treehouse *and* your own room!"

"Mama won't let me *sleep* in the treehouse," Oliver said. "She worries too much."

"Like mother, like daughter," Uncle Arthur noted. "Can you pass me another taco?"

Mama snatched the taco platter away from her brother. "Excuse me! I am not like her *at all.*"

"Uh-huh," Uncle Arthur teased.

Mama narrowed her eyes at her brother, then looked at her son. "Oliver, you can sleep in the treehouse once it's done *and* I have personally inspected it. Also, it has to be good weather. How's that? How many cool-mom points do I get?"

Oliver was so shocked, he dropped his taco. The shell cracked and the filling fell out onto his plate.

"Can I sleep in Oliver's room when he sleeps in the treehouse?" Laney asked.

Hyacinth's head popped up. "Why do you want your own room all of a sudden? I thought you liked being roommates."

Laney tilted her head, considering. "I do like it. I just want to see what it feels like. Aurelia and Zelalem and Jake all have their own rooms. They say it's the best."

Oliver again regained his powers of speech. "Does that mean . . . I could sleep in the treehouse . . . tonight?"

Mama glanced at Uncle Arthur.

"Not tonight, bud," Uncle Arthur said. "But I think we'll be done by tomorrow."

Oliver pumped a fist in the air. "Can I invite Angie?"

"Sure," Mama said. "As long as Mr. Smiley says it's okay."

"Can Jimmy L come too?"

"As long as his mom says it's okay," Mama agreed.

"What about Herman Huxley?" Hyacinth asked.

Oliver shook his head. "His dad would never let him sleep over in a million years."

The rest of the Vanderbeeker kids nodded. After they had singlehandedly destroyed Mr. Huxley's dreams of building a multimillion-dollar condominium on the land next to the church last summer, Mr. Huxley disliked the Vanderbeekers with a passion and even forbade his son Herman to hang out with them. That meant Hyacinth and Oliver, who liked Herman very much, only got to spend time with him at school.

"Sleeping in the treehouse! Wow. Can I be excused?" Oliver said, pushing his chair out and getting up from the table. "I've got to tell Angie and Jimmy L."

"You're welcome!" Mama said.

Oliver ran to his mom and hugged her. "Thank you!

You're the best mom ever!" And then he ran to the backyard to tell his friends. Laney knew all about their "secret" ways of communicating. Oliver would use his walkie-talkie to tell Jimmy L, who lived right behind their brownstone. Then he would write a note to Angie and pin it to their clothesline note-sharing system, which went from their backyard to Angie's bedroom window.

Meanwhile, Mama reached under the table to pet a kitten that had fallen asleep using her foot as a pillow. "I could get used to having more pets around," she said. "It makes the brownstone feel cozy."

Laney's heart leaped in hopefulness—maybe Mama would let her keep the tuxedo cat *and* the guinea pigs!—and then she felt someone kick her under the table. She looked up and saw Jessie looking at her and giving a little shake of her head. Laney slumped back down in her chair. No more pets, because of Mama's license.

Sometimes the universe had lousy timing.

❋ ❋ ❋

As the Vanderbeekers were cleaning up after dinner, the doorbell rang. No one was expecting a visitor, and when they opened the door, they found Cassandra standing outside.

"Hi!" Cassandra said. "Surprise!"

"I'm not surprised!" Laney said. "I knew you would come."

"I'm surprised," Papa said, looking at her mermaid hair. "Who are you?"

Cassandra stuck out a hand. "I'm Cassandra, veterinarian-in-training at Central Harlem Animal Hospital."

"She gave the kittens their shots," Hyacinth told Papa.

"So we have *you* to thank for these kittens," Papa said.

"Yes, sir," Cassandra said. "My parents were so proud to see me finally treating patients. 'Took long enough,' my dad told me. Then he asked whether I was going to start paying back my college loans anytime soon. Anyway, I wanted to come and see how the little sweethearts are doing."

The Vanderbeekers welcomed her inside. Cassandra stopped to exclaim over the fuchsia paint job. "Dr. Singh should totally paint our office that color!" she exclaimed. Then she kneeled down to examine the kittens.

"I thought they just got checkups yesterday," Mama said.

"Better safe than sorry," Cassandra explained. After she was satisfied that the kittens were healthy, she showed the Vanderbeekers how to give them full-body massages.

"It helps them be comfortable with people," Cassandra said, using her fingertips to rub little circles on their bellies. "I should make a YouTube video about how to do this."

The kittens loved this new experience, and they rumbled with satisfaction as the kids followed Cassandra's instructions. Her work done, Cassandra packed her stethoscope back into her purse. Mama gave her a bag of double chocolate pecan cookies as a thank-you gift, and Cassandra said goodbye.

The Vanderbeeker kids carried the sleepy, post-massage kittens upstairs.

"What are we going to do with these guys on Thursday?" Oliver asked as he watched the kittens get settled into the crate.

"Cassandra said we could call on Thursday morning and see if there was space in their adoption area by then," Jessie said. "The inspection isn't until three thirty, so we have time in the morning."

"And if that doesn't work?" Oliver persisted.

"I asked Mr. Beiderman about watching the pets," Hyacinth informed them. "He said he'd take Franz, George Washington, and Paganini, but he didn't seem very happy about it. He definitely doesn't want the kittens or guinea pigs."

Oliver fiddled with his basketball, throwing it up in the air and catching it as it fell. "So we really need to get them adopted."

"I am *not* going back to the Animal Care Center," Jessie declared.

Isa picked up her phone. "I wonder if anyone answered our adoption advertisement yet." She opened her email and found two messages. She read the first one out loud. " 'I saw your ad for kittens. Would you be interested in a joint venture where we train the kittens for the circus?' "

"Yes!" Laney said, jumping up and down. "Tell that person yes!"

Oliver agreed with Laney. "That would be cool. A cat circus. Nice."

"No way," Hyacinth said. "Those cats deserve to live their lives in peace, not working for the circus!"

"That email sounds shady," Jessie said. "Delete it."

Laney slumped in disappointment.

"Here's the second one," Isa said, "from a Mrs. Swallowbee. 'Keep up the marvelous work!!! Trap, Neuter, Release Forever!!!' "

"What does that even mean?" Oliver asked.

"It's for cats that live on the streets," Jessie explained. "People capture them and give them a surgery so they can't have kittens, then release them back into the neighborhood."

"That's sad they can't have babies," Laney said, sticking her fingers into the cage and petting the head of the tuxedo cat. "I love kittens."

Jessie sighed. "I was hoping that people who wanted to *adopt* them would email us. And no interest in the guinea pigs at all."

"The flyers have only been up for a few hours," Isa pointed out before leaving. "I'm sure we'll get more emails tomorrow."

Laney and Hyacinth changed into their pajamas, and Papa arrived to read a chapter of *The Trumpet of the Swan* to them, making sure he really exaggerated all the parts when Louis's father was talking. A few minutes after he began reading, Laney's soft snores came through the pile of blankets she had buried herself under. When Papa finished the chapter, Hyacinth declared his read-aloud performance a "masterpiece." He took a bow, kissed his daughters on the cheek, and checked on the kittens. Then he patted Franz on the head and called him a good dog and plugged in the night-light before going downstairs to hang out with Mama.

Hyacinth curled up against the crate, and Franz snuggled on her other side. She fell asleep to the sound of the kittens' whispered breathing, Franz's rumbling snores, and the guinea pigs taking turns on the exercise wheel. Hours later, when the last Vanderbeeker fell asleep, the brownstone finally settled down for the night with a contented creak, wrapping the family and their ten animals safely in its embrace for another day.

APRIL

MONDAY	TUESDAY	WEDNESDAY
1	2	3
	Find homes for kittens!	Find homes for kittens and guinea pigs!

← S·P·R·I·N·G

Wednesday, April 3

THURSDAY	FRIDAY	SATURDAY
4	5	6
3:30 p.m. Inspection	Perch Magazine Photo Shoot!	Mama's Birthday!
	Isa's Audition	
B·R·E·A·K	→	→

Eighteen

Jessie woke up the next morning to the sound of barking.

Lots of barking.

She opened her eyes and wondered what it might be like to wake up to the rustle of leaves in the wind, or birdsong, or maybe even silence for once in her life.

Isa must have stayed up late again the previous night, because she was fast asleep despite the barking. Jessie threw on her mom's old college sweatshirt, then left her bedroom to investigate.

Stepping into the hallway, she ran right into Laney, Oliver, and Hyacinth with a frantic and loud Franz. Their parents' door opened, and Mama and Papa stood in the doorway, their eyes heavy with sleep.

"What's the racket?" Papa asked, rubbing his hair so it stood up even more than usual.

Meanwhile, Franz was barking and running in circles. He tugged at the bottom of Hyacinth's pajama shirt before letting go and racing down the stairs. They followed him and found him pawing at the back door.

When Hyacinth looked out the door windows, she saw a medium-sized dog with short reddish-brown hair and white fur on the tips of its paws. The dog had a fresh cut across its nose, and at the sight of the six Vanderbeekers through the window, its stub of a tail wagged tentatively.

Hyacinth looked up at her parents. "Can I go outside?"

"Absolutely not," Mama said at the same time Papa said, "Yes."

Hyacinth's eyes bounced between them.

"We mean yes, you can go out with adult supervision," Papa amended.

The rest of the Vanderbeekers backed up so Papa could open the door. Jessie held Franz's collar, and Hyacinth stepped toward the dog outside and squatted to let it sniff her hand. The dog dipped its head and licked her fingers.

Papa turned around and gave Mama a thumbs-up, and the other Vanderbeekers tumbled out the door. Franz scrambled to reach the new dog, but Jessie kept a firm grip on his collar.

"First the kittens, then guinea pigs, now a dog." Papa shook his head but reached down to pet the new dog. "Whew, this dog smells."

"This animal thing is getting out of hand," Jessie said. "What is going on?"

"I think we should name her Frida, after Frida Kahlo," Hyacinth said, wetting a paper towel to wipe the dirt around the cut on her nose.

"We're not naming them, remember?" Jessie said.

"I think we should name her Ginger Pye," Laney said, ignoring Jessie. "Like the dog in the book Mama read to me."

"WE ARE NOT NAMING THEM!" Jessie bellowed.

Everyone froze. When Jessie got upset, she usually rolled her eyes, or stomped, or pouted. Very rarely did she yell.

But as much as Oliver tried to resist, he couldn't help himself. "Don't you think she looks more like a Beyoncé?"

* * *

After showing the-dog-that-must-not-have-a-name around the apartment, Hyacinth set out breakfast for the dogs while the rest of the Vanderbeekers fed the kittens, George Washington, the guinea pigs, and Paganini. New Dog, as Jessie made everyone call her, was not interested in eating, so after Franz finished his bowl, he sat staring at the second bowl of food. Hyacinth warned him not to touch it, but when she went to the bathroom to brush her teeth, Franz helped himself to a second breakfast. New Dog didn't mind. She went back and forth between Franz and the kittens, offering the occasional tail wag when someone walked by and scratched behind her ears.

Immediately following breakfast, the Vanderbeekers retreated to Oliver's bedroom to talk about this emergency development. Isa had been dragged out of bed to consult on the issue, and now they were crammed into Oliver's narrow room with all the animals except Paganini, who was not allowed in the bedrooms because of his tendency to chew mattresses. Jessie handed Isa a smoothie.

"We need to get to the bottom of this," Jessie said. "We have five kittens, two guinea pigs, and now *a dog.*"

"Who is leaving these animals?" Isa wondered, stifling a yawn as she spoke.

"I'm making a list of suspects." Oliver pulled out his notebook and a magnifying glass. He held the magnifying glass up to New Dog's face, and New Dog instantly licked it. "Ugh, your breath stinks," Oliver said to her.

"It's got to be someone who knows us," Jessie said. "Someone who knows we're an animal family."

"I still think it's someone who hates us," Oliver said, wiping the magnifying glass with the bottom of his shirt. "Someone who wants to sabotage Mama's business."

"What's 'sabotage'?" Laney asked.

"It's when someone purposely does something to get you in trouble," Oliver said.

Isa spoke up. "Oliver, no one besides us knows about the inspection. They can't sabotage it if they didn't even know about it." She yawned again.

“I’m putting Mr. West’s name down,” Oliver said. “Also Mr. Huxley.”

“No way it’s either of them,” Jessie said.

“Maybe it’s someone who likes us and knows that we love animals,” Hyacinth said. “Like Triple J, or Mr. Jones.” Triple J was the pastor of the church down the street, and Mr. Jones was their postman. “Maybe the animals had really bad owners, and Triple J and Mr. Jones rescued them and brought them to us for safekeeping.”

“That doesn’t make sense,” Oliver said. “Why would they leave the animals outside in boxes instead of just knocking on the door and asking?”

Jessie sighed. “*Your* suspects didn’t make sense either.”

Oliver made a face at her, but he wrote the names down anyway.

“How about that guy who puts his Chihuahuas in sweaters?” Isa suggested. “He’s always struck me as a little strange.”

“His name,” Hyacinth said, “is Mr. Greenwillow, and his Chihuahuas’ names are Barry and Francisco.”

"Um, okay," Oliver said. "Should I write him down, or . . ."

"Yes," Isa said at the same time Hyacinth said, "No."

"So are we just writing down anyone who lives in the neighborhood now?" Oliver said.

"Everyone is a suspect," Jessie said, her eyes landing on her brother. "Even you."

"Me?" Oliver said, pointing to himself. "I'm innocent!"

"Or are you?" Jessie said, gesturing to his notebook. "Go on, write your name on the list."

"Oh, come on," Oliver said, throwing his pencil to the floor.

"This isn't getting us anywhere," Isa said, pulling out her phone. "Let me check and see if anyone emailed us about the animals. If we have any takers, maybe Allegra can make a poster for New Dog—" Isa stopped as she scrolled through her emails. "Oh no."

"What?" said Jessie, Oliver, Hyacinth, and Laney.

"It's an email from the City of New York," Isa said slowly. "Apparently our flyers violate section ten-one nineteen of New York City's Administrative Code. The Department of Sanitation has removed six of them, and each one is a seventy-five-dollar fine."

"Are you telling me," Jessie said after doing a quick calculation in her head, "that we owe the City of New York four hundred and fifty dollars?"

Isa looked up from her phone. "That's exactly what I'm saying."

Nineteen

The Vanderbeekers put the kittens back into their crate, then raced out of the apartment, dragging Franz and New Dog with them. They had to find the rest of the flyers they had put up, and they had to do it fast. They'd hung some in windows of businesses, which apparently did not warrant a fine, but that left thirty-six copies out there. If the Department of Sanitation found them before the Vanderbeekers did, it would add up to a fine of $2,700.

Hyacinth let Franz smell a copy of the one flyer they had kept, then said, "Go find the rest, Franz!" Franz howled and immediately pulled her leash in the direction of the park.

"I think he has a lead!" Hyacinth said, running after him.

Franz zigzagged his way in the direction of St. Nicholas Park, and soon the Vanderbeekers realized that Franz just wanted to chase squirrels, because they definitely hadn't put any flyers in that area. They backtracked to 141st Street and headed south, retracing their steps to the library. They'd found twenty-four flyers by the time they reached 138th Street, and as they passed Harlem Coffee, they saw Herman Huxley come out.

"Herman!" Hyacinth and Oliver said. They hadn't seen him since school let out for spring break.

Herman's face broke into a wide grin, and then he spotted the flyers in their hands. "Hey, are you the ones with the kittens? I've seen these flyers everywhere. Is that a new dog?"

"We found five kittens outside our brownstone two days ago and two guinea pigs yesterday, and today this dog showed up," Hyacinth said. "Someone is leaving them, but we need them all out of our house by tomorrow morning. Do you want to adopt them?"

"Of course I do!" He leaned down to pet New Dog. "Whew, this dog smells."

"You can't have the tuxedo cat," Laney told him. "That one is mine."

"Don't mind Laney. She doesn't know what she's talking about," Jessie said quickly. She pushed her leash into Herman's hand. "You can take New Dog now and then follow us back to our apartment and pick up the kittens, okay?"

Herman handed the leash back to Jessie. "Are you kidding? I *wish* I could have them all, but my dad would never let me get pets. Never."

"Well, thanks a lot, Herman," Jessie said with a huff. "You've been supremely unhelpful."

"No time to chat," Isa said, grabbing Laney's hand and moving on. "We need to find all the flyers before we get another fine. There are twelve more out there." The twins rushed off to look, dragging Laney behind them. Hyacinth, Herman, Oliver, and the dogs followed at a less frantic pace.

Hyacinth looked at Herman, then back at the coffee shop. "Were you getting . . . coffee?"

Herman was wearing his backpack, which looked loaded down with something heavy. "My dad is on this publicity kick. He's making me go around to different buildings and businesses to pass out these postcards." He gave her a card bearing a photo of Mr. Huxley, his arms crossed over his chest, looming in front of a luxury condominium.

"That sounds terrible," Oliver said, "although passing out postcards sounds better than the trouble we're in right now."

"Wait, what trouble?" Herman asked as he reached up and plucked two flyers off a lamppost.

Oliver and Hyacinth alternated telling the story. When they were done, there was a long pause. Then Herman let out a low whistle.

"Wow," Herman said. "I'm so glad I'm not you right now."

❋ ❋ ❋

Oliver, Hyacinth, and Herman met up with the rest of the Vanderbeekers in front of the library. Isa, Jessie, and Laney had found six additional flyers, and Herman, Oliver, and Hyacinth had found three, so they were missing just one.

"Where could it be?" Isa fretted.

"It's just one flyer," Oliver said. "Let's go home. I'm so hungry!"

Jessie glared at her brother. "Do *you* want to pay the seventy-five dollars for that flyer?"

Oliver calculated the amount of allowance it would take to save up seventy-five dollars; then he shook his head.

"Let's go home anyway," Hyacinth suggested. "Maybe we'll see the last one on our way."

The Vanderbeekers and Herman weaved their way home, using exactly the same route they had taken the day before. They went back past Harlem Coffee, which now had a line out the door with people needing caffeine, then past bodegas, their windows displaying candy, dish detergent, and cereal. At 141st Street, they made a right and went by the church and the community garden. Because of the abundant spring rain, there were plenty of weeds poking through the ground, and Oliver dreaded the day his sisters suggested they do a garden cleanup.

The last flyer was nowhere to be found.

"Fine, forget it," Jessie finally said. "We need to do

some serious, on-the-ground promotion today. Here's what I'm thinking: let's get pets on the wagon and walk around the neighborhood. We don't come home until they're all adopted."

Oliver couldn't think of a worse way to spend the day, especially since it was a treehouse-building day, but Mr. West *was* coming back tomorrow, and they had to solve the animal problem.

"We still need to paint the living room," Isa pointed out. "And Oliver needs to work on the treehouse while Uncle Arthur is free."

Oliver shot Isa a grateful look, then pledged to compliment her violin playing every chance he got.

"Okay, what about this?" Jessie suggested. "You and Oliver prime and paint the living room, and I'll take Hyacinth and Laney with me."

"I'll go with you too," Herman said.

"Yay!" Hyacinth and Laney said.

It was eleven o'clock by the time they made it back to the brownstone. Uncle Arthur was sitting on the steps with four cans of primer around him.

"I thought we were meeting at ten thirty," Uncle

Arthur said to Oliver. "Oh, hey, Herman. Wait, is that a new dog?"

"Yup, this is New Dog," Oliver said, leading her on the leash toward him.

"Wait, the new dog's name is New Dog?" Uncle Arthur asked.

"It's a name *and* a description," Laney told him.

Herman spoke up. "Don't you think it's a terrible injustice that they have eleven pets and I have none?"

"Yes," Uncle Arthur said.

"Eight of these animals don't belong to us," Oliver clarified.

Herman didn't respond.

"I've got the primer," Uncle Arthur said, putting his hands on top of the cans. "Should we get to work?"

"Yes! Painting! Yes!" Laney chanted.

Jessie stepped in. "Laney, we're not going to paint. We're going to get the animals adopted, okay?"

"But not Tuxedo, right?"

Jessie hesitated, which Laney took as a good sign. She was already on her way into the brownstone, yelling, "Tuxedo! Where are you, girl? We're going on a wagon ride!"

"Great job," Oliver said to Jessie. "She totally thinks Tuxedo belongs to her now."

"And that," Jessie told him, "is why we don't name pets we can't keep."

Twenty

It was decided that Jessie and Laney should bathe New Dog first (they determined there was a higher possibility of her being adopted if she smelled like freesia and lemon instead of a garbage dump) while Hyacinth and Herman worked on making the wagon eye-catching. They made a big poster and used some of Hyacinth's knitted yarn accessories to decorate it.

When they were done, they went back inside to check on the bath progress. Franz, who had been with Hyacinth, got one glimpse of the filled bathtub and bolted upstairs to

hide under the bunk bed. He did not like baths.

Hyacinth peeked into the bathroom. Laney was wearing a bathing suit and goggles and was in the tub with New Dog. Bubbles were flowing over the edge and onto the bathmat. Unlike Franz, New Dog appeared to love baths and was even letting Laney give her a bubble beard and bubble hair.

Jessie was sitting on the closed toilet seat scribbling wildly in her science notebook. "If I used tubes to dispense the food—"

"What's that?" Hyacinth said, reading over Jessie's shoulder. The words at the top of her notebook said, "Rube Goldberg Kitten-Feeding Machine."

Jessie looked up and surveyed the bathroom. "Jeez, Laney, you made a huge mess!" She pulled a towel down from the hook.

"Are you going to make that machine?" Hyacinth said, pointing at her notebook.

Jessie nodded. "Science fair project."

New Dog shook herself off, spraying everyone with water and bubbles. Jessie snapped her notebook shut, shoved it in her back jeans pocket, then wrapped New

Dog in a fresh towel. Hyacinth helped Laney shower off, then get dressed, but no one could convince her to give up the goggles. They leashed the dogs, and off they went.

The air was crisp, and the sky was a clear blue. They rolled the adoption wagon along 141st Street, under trees that were hundreds of years old and over roots that caused the sidewalk to buckle. The merry chirps of birds filled the air, and the kittens were awake and alert, their eyes wide with wonder.

First they stopped to see Cassandra at the Central Harlem Animal Hospital. She took a selfie with the kittens ("They look better than yesterday! Great job!"), complimented Laney on her goggles, examined New Dog, checked her for a microchip that would show her owner's information if scanned by the vet (she didn't have one), and got her up-to-date on her immunizations. Cassandra thought the guinea pigs looked fine, although she admitted she wasn't qualified to provide veterinary care to them. Finally, she gave the Vanderbeekers the bad news: there was still no space in the adoption center for the kittens.

"But they need to be out by tomorrow morning," Jessie pleaded. "Is there any way for you to take them until tomorrow afternoon?"

"I'm sorry," Cassandra told them. "If I could, I would."

The Vanderbeekers said goodbye and set off into Harlem. Surely there had to be people in the neighborhood who could provide the perfect home for these pets.

❊ ❊ ❊

Three hours later, Laney was still full of energy. She loved talking to people—it was pretty much her favorite thing to do—and when they went by the park, she saw a group of her friends from kindergarten and got to show off the kittens and guinea pigs. Every one of her friends wanted to adopt them—of course they did!—but their parents and caretakers said no.

All day long Laney had crossed her fingers and secretly hoped that no one would be interested in Tuxedo, and she might have been wishing a little *too* hard, because in the end no one wanted to adopt *any* of the animals. Laney could tell that Jessie was getting more and more worried as the afternoon went on.

"I'll have to think about it," said a woman wearing jeans, black boots, and a leather jacket. She liked the gray kitten. "I live with three roommates, and I need to get permission from everyone first."

"I'm allergic," said another man, and as if to prove his point, he gave an enormous sneeze, which startled New Dog so much that her tail went down and she squeezed herself under the wagon to hide.

"I've got my hands full," said a mom who was wrangling a set of triplet boys who looked a lot younger than Laney. "Also, I don't think a kitten would be safe around these guys." Even though she looked frazzled, she shot her kids an affectionate smile.

When they walked by an assisted-living community, seven people were sitting along the sidewalk in wheelchairs, their faces tilted toward the sun. The sound of the wagon jolted them from their daydreams, and they looked with interest at the animal parade.

"What have you got there?" asked a gentleman wearing multiple layers of clothes and a hat.

"They're kittens, Charles," said the lady next to him. "And hamsters." She wore glasses at the tip of her nose.

"Those aren't hamsters; they're guinea pigs," piped up another woman. She had her hair in curlers and a shower cap. "Bring them here."

Jessie rolled the wagon over, and the woman in curlers leaned down to peer at the guinea pigs.

"Hand me a kitten," said another woman, and Herman opened the crate and picked up a kitten for her to hold. Pretty soon five of them were holding kittens, and another woman had one hand on New Dog and one on Franz.

"Anyone want to adopt a kitten, guinea pig, or dog?" Jessie asked them, but no one responded. Their hands were on the animals, and they were all smiling.

"Reminds me of my first cat," said the woman in the curlers. "Her name was Tiger. She was beautiful."

"Mine was Rufus Mulligan the Third," said the man with the hat. "He slept under the covers with me."

"I had a cat who liked to walk on a leash," said another woman. "Everyone knew us, and the storekeeper on 137th Street would give her treats when we passed by. That was a real nice cat."

"My granddaughter has a hamster," said the woman petting the dogs.

"Those are guinea pigs!" corrected the person next to her, pointing at the cage.

Laney figured that none of these people could adopt a pet right now—they looked as if they needed a lot of help just taking care of themselves—but she was glad they could be with the animals for a little bit. A few minutes later, someone from the nursing home came out and said it was time for everyone to come in. Jessie, Hyacinth, and Herman collected the kittens and put them back into their box, and Laney gave out goodbye hugs. The residents waved as staff emerged from the building and began wheeling the people back in.

"Come back and visit," they said as they were rolled up the ramp. "And bring the animals with you!"

* * *

The sun was beginning to set when Jessie, Hyacinth, Laney, and Herman left the retirement home.

"What are we going to do with the animals?" Jessie fretted. "We have gotten exactly zero pets adopted. Why is this so hard?" She thought about the $450 fine;

it might be up to $525 now, if the Department of Sanitation had found the last flyer. They had spent all their money buying the paint so they didn't have to dip into the Fiver Account, and Jessie couldn't bear to tell her parents that they now needed hundreds of dollars because they had violated a city code.

Herman, who was walking in front of the wagon, stopped, and Jessie almost ran into him.

"Maybe I can help with the kittens," he said, turning around to face Jessie, Hyacinth, and Laney.

"How?" Jessie asked.

"My dad has some kind of Realtors' banquet tonight until super late. Tomorrow he leaves early to go to Brooklyn for a conference. So . . . maybe I can bring them home with me?"

"If your dad finds out," Hyacinth said, "he will *flip*."

Herman stood up as straight as the lamppost he was next to. "He's not going to find out. I know exactly where I'll hide them."

"You'll take extra-good care of Tuxedo, right?" Laney asked.

Jessie looked at Herman. "Are you sure? Like, one hundred percent sure?"

"Sure I'm sure," Herman said. "Just drop them off now, and then come back tomorrow after the inspection to pick them up. And you should ask Angie to take the guinea pigs. She loves guinea pigs."

The Vanderbeekers went home to drop off the guinea pigs and pick up kitten food and the litterbox; then they brought the kittens and the supplies to Herman's house in the wagon. He didn't want them to come up to his apartment—his bedroom was a huge mess, he told them—so they gave the kittens goodbye kisses and loaded the cat crate and supplies into the elevator. Then they waved until the elevator door closed and whisked the kittens up to Herman's apartment.

Twenty-One

When Jessie, Hyacinth, and Laney returned home after dropping the kittens off at Herman's place, they found Oliver in a great mood. His treehouse was done, his sleepover was about to begin, and the living room walls were painted white and looked as awesome as boring white walls could look. When Laney told him that the kittens had a home for the night, Oliver was so thrilled that she asked if she could sleep in his room and he said yes!

Laney couldn't wait to finally experience a night of sleeping in a room alone. After dinner, she moved all her stuffed animals into Oliver's room and fluffed up his blanket to her standard of comfort.

When she left his room to go say good night to everyone, she bumped into Hyacinth, who was coming out of their shared bedroom with Franz.

"We get our own rooms tonight!" Laney said to Hyacinth.

"Great," Hyacinth said.

Laney frowned, not knowing why Hyacinth didn't seem as excited about this arrangement as she was. She headed down the stairs to find the rest of her siblings—plus Angie and Jimmy L—outside, huddled around the grill making s'mores. She stepped outside, and Isa handed her a graham-cracker sandwich filled with gooey marshmallows and melted chocolate.

"Guess what?" Oliver said to his siblings as they settled out on the grass and ate the sticky dessert. "Angie said she can take care of the guinea pigs tomorrow when the inspector is here."

Everyone cheered.

Angie smiled and gave a pump of her arms toward the sky. "I'll take them with me after the sleepover."

"Aren't you scared about sleeping out here?" Hyacinth asked Oliver.

"Nope," Oliver said. "Jessie hooked up an emergency bell if we need anything." He pointed up, and Hyacinth saw a red string that went from the treehouse right to Mama and Papa's bedroom, which faced the backyard. "We just pull the string and it rings a bell in Mama and Papa's bedroom."

Hyacinth eyed it with skepticism.

"It works like the bus," Jessie explained. "You know that yellow cord that goes across the windows? You pull on it when you want to get off at the next stop? Same mechanism."

"No one comes back here anyway," Oliver assured her.

"And Mama and Papa's room is literally twenty feet away from the treehouse," Jessie added.

"What about the person who keeps leaving the animals here?" Hyacinth asked. She looked around, just in case someone was lurking in the darkness.

"Ooh," Angie said. "We should set up a video camera so we can catch the person!"

Jessie's eyes lit up. "That's a great idea! Papa has that flip video thing that he won from his office party a couple of years ago. I'll get it! I know where he keeps

TREEHOUSE ALARM SYSTEM
In case of emergency, pull string.
Mama & Papa's Bedroom

it." She ran inside the brownstone, and Isa lay down on the ground, looking up into the universe. Laney copied her, but there were no stars to be seen in that square patch of sky bordered by buildings.

Jessie came back with the flip recorder, and they turned it on to see if it worked. Oliver mugged for the camera, and they played it back. While the image was a little dark, they could still tell it was Oliver. Jessie, Oliver, Angie, and Jimmy L climbed the ladder to set up the camera. They got the angle perfect and secured it using a combination of string and masking tape.

"We're going to catch this animal-leaver person!" yelled Oliver from the treehouse, giving them a thumbs-up.

"He's no match for us!" Jimmy L proclaimed. Then he stood up too fast when he was withdrawing from the treehouse and bumped his head on the top of the window. Angie burst into giggles.

Hyacinth winced as she and her sisters headed inside. "Are they going to be okay out here all by themselves?"

"They're fine," Isa said. "A little dopey, but they'll be okay."

❊ ❊ ❊

Oliver had never been to sleep-away camp, but he imagined it would be something like this treehouse sleepover. So far, everything had been awesome. They'd had a chin-up competition (Angie won, by a lot), seen how many marshmallows they could fit in their mouths at once (Jimmy L won, by a lot), and scratched their names into the treehouse wall with an X-Acto knife.

Oliver grabbed a graham cracker and munched on it while they played Quiddler, a card game Angie was obsessed with.

"I wish I could adopt one of the kittens," Angie said as she drew a card and analyzed her hand. "Lucky Herman."

"He's not adopting them," Oliver said. "He's just watching them until tomorrow. Anyway, you're watching the guinea pigs."

Jimmy L put a card down. "But I thought you're not

supposed to have *any* pets if you want your mom to keep the license. So aren't you breaking the rules if the animals are just being moved temporarily?"

Oliver shrugged. "Right now we're in crisis-management mode until the photo shoot. Once we're done with that, we'll figure out a permanent solution."

"Does that mean you'll give away your pets, too?"

"No," Oliver said. "We have a lot to figure out."

"Hey," Angie said, "remember when my Aunt Eva took me out for my birthday last month? We went to a cat café in Brooklyn. It's like a regular coffee shop, but it also had all these adoptable cats roaming around. Maybe you should bring the kittens there to get adopted."

"That's a good idea," Oliver said. "Too bad Brooklyn is a million miles away."

"Sixteen miles," Angie corrected him.

"It feels like a million," Oliver grumbled. "The last time we went to Brooklyn, the subways were all messed up and it took two hours to get home."

They finished the game. No one wanted to be the first to admit that they were tired, but Oliver was starting to feel drowsy. He peeked out the north window and saw that the lights were still on in Jimmy L's apartment. It looked as if his mom was washing the dishes, and as she passed by the window, she peeked through, probably to see whether they were sleeping yet. Then, as if all the parents had planned it, he heard a couple of doors and a window open.

"Oliver!" Papa called from the back door.

"Angie!" Mr. Smiley said from the basement of the building two doors down.

"Jimmy!" said his mom from the open window across the way.

"Yeah?" they answered, hopping up and looking out the respective windows in the direction of their parents' voices.

"Time for bed!" the parents hollered in unison.

Oliver, Angie, and Jimmy L put up a little bit of a fight, but Oliver was secretly relieved to crawl into his sleeping bag. The floor was hard, and he wondered why he hadn't thought to bring up another blanket to sleep on top of. Next to him, Angie was wearing a thick sweatshirt and a knit hat. The spring night was cool, and it made Oliver look forward to summer sleepovers.

"Your uncle should put a skylight in here," Angie said. "That would be awesome."

"Yeah," Jimmy L said. "Like, Treehouse 2.0."

"I'll ask," Oliver murmured. He burrowed down into his sleeping bag and pulled his hoodie over his head for warmth. In minutes, Jimmy L was already breathing deeply, and because of previous experience at sleepovers, Oliver knew it was only a matter of time before his friend started snoring. He glanced up at the video camera to double-check that the recording light was on; then he drifted off with the sound of the wind whistling through the trees, the chatter of a noisy group of teenagers walking down the street, the distant sound of a dog whimpering . . .

❊ ❊ ❊

Isa was having an awful time falling asleep. Even though they had repainted the walls, found a temporary home for Franz, George Washington, Paganini, the guinea pigs, and the kittens, and confirmed that

Mama would be out of the brownstone during the inspection (she was taking a website-creation workshop downtown so she could redesign her baking website), there were many things to worry about. They still didn't know what to do about New Dog; plus there was that enormous fine from the illegal flyers *and* she had the audition coming up.

She sat up and looked across the room at Jessie. It was fairly early, but her sister had crawled into bed and crashed immediately, probably because she was exhausted from running around Harlem for the past two days and taking care of their siblings and the new pets.

Since she was wide awake, Isa figured she might as well practice. The next morning would be busy with cleaning the apartment, moving the pets, and getting ready for the inspection. She swung her legs off the side of the bed and left the bedroom.

She was about to head downstairs when she heard Laney whimpering. Peeking into Laney and Hyacinth's bedroom, she momentarily panicked when she saw that the bottom bunk was empty. Another sob coming from the room next door made Isa remember that Laney was in Oliver's room, and Oliver was in the treehouse. She stepped into Oliver's closet-sized bedroom, and there was Laney, sitting at the edge of the loft bed and clutching her stuffed rabbit, Babo.

Isa reached over and picked up her little sister, and Laney wrapped her arms and legs around Isa.

"I don't like sleeping by myself either," Isa confided to Laney.

"Hyacinth protects me from the monsters," Laney said, and sniffled.

"And Jessie protects me," Isa told her. "Isn't it great to have sisters? Why don't I bring you back to bed, okay?"

Laney nodded. "Will you bring my stuffed animals?"

Isa smiled. "Of course." Isa dropped Laney off in her bedroom, where Laney promptly burrowed herself inside her blanket cave. Then Isa went back for all the stuffed animals and settled them around her sister. She kissed Laney's forehead and scratched Franz behind the ears, then went downstairs to find that

Papa had fallen asleep on the couch, a book on his chest. She tiptoed past him and descended into the basement, mentally preparing herself for another night of practice.

APRIL

MONDAY	TUESDAY	WEDNESDAY
1	2 Find homes for kittens!	3 Find homes for kittens and guinea pigs!
←	S·	P·R·I·N·G

Thursday, April 4

THURSDAY
4
:30 p.m. Drop off animals at Mr. B's
:30 p.m. Inspection
B·R·E·A·K

FRIDAY
5
Perch Magazine Photo Shoot!
Isa's Audition

SATURDAY
6
Mama's Birthday!

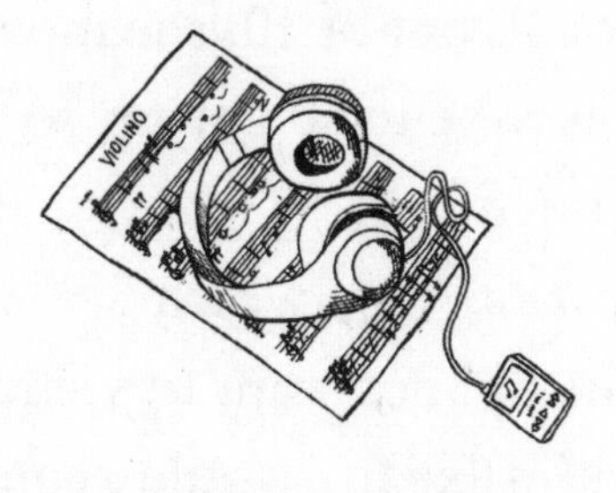

Twenty-Two

The next morning, Laney woke up in her bed with Babo on her face. She could hear Hyacinth's gentle breathing from the bunk above her, and it made her so relieved to be back in her own bunk and not all by herself in Oliver's room. She moved the stuffed rabbit off her face and emerged from her tunnel of blankets. Her eyes immediately went in search of the kittens, and it took her a moment after looking at the empty spot where the crate had been to remember that Herman was taking care of them. The guinea pig cage was on top of her dresser, and the animals were cuddled up next to each other, fast asleep.

Laney crawled out of bed, trying not to disturb her perfect blanket setup. Whenever she had her bed at a comfort level of 10 out of 10, she moved the covers as little as possible when she got up so she could crawl right back in at bedtime.

It was inspection day, which she was *not* looking forward to—she did not want to see Mr. West again—but afterward, Tuxedo would come home! And tomorrow was the photo shoot, and Laney loved being photographed. She couldn't wait to see herself in the glossy magazine.

It was time to pick out the perfect outfit. Laney closed her eyes and tried to think of the best thing in the world, and the first thing that came to mind was unicorns. She opened the dresser she shared with Hyacinth and rummaged through her clothes until she found her favorite unicorn shirt, her rainbow leggings, and the best socks for sliding in: the white ones with gold stars. In the closet she searched for her red cowboy boots, which had been owned by each of her sisters before her, and her cousins before them. Those boots had a lot of magic from being worn by so many people.

On the top bunk, Hyacinth awoke and stretched.

As she leaned over the railing, Laney waved and Franz barked a good morning, his tail wagging at 120 wpm. Hyacinth grinned at the sight of them.

"I dreamed about kittens last night," Laney told her. "They were wearing scarves and doing synchronized swimming. They got gold medals."

Hyacinth made her way down from the top bunk. "Nice."

Laney pulled her shirt over her head and put her arms out. "Guess my outfit theme."

"Easy," Hyacinth said. "Unicorn power. But you need one last flourish." She pulled a bin from under Laney's bed and removed a headband with long ribbons in every color of the rainbow tied to it. She set it on Laney's head and stepped back to examine the finished product.

"Perfect," Hyacinth said.

Laney gave Hyacinth a hug. "I love being roommates with you."

"I love being roommates with you, too," Hyacinth said.

While Hyacinth got dressed, Laney pranced to the

bedroom at the end of the hall to see if her other sisters were awake. Isa was asleep, but her headphones were still on; she was drooling on a stack of sheet music. New Dog had slept at her side; her eyes opened and her tail wagged at Laney's entrance. Jessie looked as if she had had an epic wrestling match with her covers during the night. The comforter was twisted into a rope and wrapped around her stomach.

Laney decided to wake Isa first, but as she was about to remove Isa's headphones, Jessie shot out of bed, took two running leaps, and slid on the floor just in time to knock Laney's hands away.

"Hey—" Laney began, but Jessie hushed her.

"Let her sleep," Jessie said in a low whisper, her finger to her lips.

Laney shrugged and followed Jessie out the door, where Jessie told her Isa had spent all night stressing about her audition. Laney stopped back in her bedroom to pick up the guinea pig cage, which she and Hyacinth carried downstairs and placed on the living room table so Angie wouldn't forget to take it with her after the sleepover.

Papa was already in the kitchen, pouring a cup of

coffee. When they came in, he kissed the tops of their heads, and Laney hugged him around the waist.

"Do you like my outfit?" Laney asked, twirling so the ribbons on her headband flew out.

"Very nice," Papa said with a smile.

Laney grinned back, then pulled a step stool over to the cupboard to reach for a box of cereal. She was on her tiptoes, the cereal nearly in reach, when a large feathery brown shape flew right into the window in front of her. Laney yelped and fell off the stool, the box of cereal slipping from her hands and showering the kitchen with puffed rice.

Papa ran over, his slippered feet crunching on the cereal. "Are you okay?"

"There's something outside!" Laney shrieked.

Papa, Hyacinth, and Jessie ran to the back door and peered out the window.

"Holy smokes," Jessie murmured under her breath.

❋ ❋ ❋

Oliver woke up to find himself fully buried in his sleeping bag. He could hear yelling from inside the brownstone, but he was so nice and warm where he was that he didn't want to get up. Just as he drifted off again, the yelling began again, accompanied by Franz's furious howling.

"What's with all the yelling?" Jimmy L muttered next to him.

Oliver emerged from his warm cocoon and sat up. Angie, who was just waking up as well, looked at him and began to laugh.

"What?" Oliver said.

"Your hair is so funny," she said, pointing.

Oliver smoothed down his hair, which was doing the normal sticking-up-in-every-direction morning thing.

"Want to see what's for breakfast?" Oliver asked, changing the subject. His friends slid out of their sleeping bags and made their way down the ladder. A shriek was heard from inside the brownstone.

"What's going on in there?" Angie asked.

"Welcome to my life," Oliver said. He jumped down the last couple of rungs, and a squawk made him startle and stumble when he landed. He rolled over and found himself face-to-face with three chickens.

"Chickens!" Angie cried.

Jimmy L, the last to come down, clung to the ladder. "I don't really like birds."

Angie picked up a chicken and cuddled it to her chest. "How can you not like chickens?"

"It's called alektorophobia," Jimmy L answered, "and it's more common than you think!"

"The animal bandit strikes again!" Oliver said. "Jimmy L, can you check the camera?"

Jimmy L scampered back up the ladder, happy to get away from the chickens, and yelled, "It's dead!"

"We'll charge it inside," Oliver told him. "Grab it and come down."

"I'm not going down there with the chickens," Jimmy L said. "They'll peck my eyes out."

"They will *not* peck your eyes out," Angie said, a chicken still in her arms.

But Jimmy L refused, and Angie and Oliver had to convince the three chickens to move to the back fence while Jimmy L rushed down the ladder and made a run for the back door. He slipped inside with Oliver and Angie behind him a few second later.

"Hey," Oliver said when he entered, spotting Papa, Jessie, and Laney clustered in the living room. "Did you know there are three chickens in our yard?" His feet crunched on a layer of cereal coating the floor. "Hey, what's with the—*ahh!*"

A large reddish-brown thing flew right at him. He and his friends ducked.

"I'm out of here!" Jimmy L yelled. Oliver sat up and watched his best friend scramble out the back door, scale the fence, and drop down into his own yard.

The brown thing came at Oliver again, and Oliver curled up on the floor atop the cereal, his hands protecting his head. Franz's barking grew even more maniacal.

"Don't just lie there—try to get it to fly this way!" Jessie yelled.

Oliver moved a hand away from his face to get a glimpse of what was attacking him. Feathers and dust were flying around his face, and he caught sight of a chicken exactly like the ones in the yard. It flapped its wings and crashed into the window on the back door. Dazed, it stood up and ran back toward the living room in wobbly circles.

"Oliver, chase it out the door!" Papa yelled.

Oliver sat up. "I'm not getting anywhere near that thing!"

Papa cast an exasperated look at him, then stepped away from where he was holding the front door open.

"I'll do it!" Angie said, and she raced toward the chicken. It dodged her easily and headed toward the basement, half jumping and half falling down the stairs. Franz, who was hiding behind the couch, continued to bark as if the world were ending.

Jessie and Angie ran down the stairs, and Oliver stayed put, because he was *not* going after that deranged chicken, no way! Papa, a more gallant man, followed them into the basement. Laney and Hyacinth went down a few steps, just enough to see the action. After what seemed like ten minutes of yelled exclamations and earsplitting squawks, Laney and Hyacinth scrambled up the stairs, yelling, "He got it!"

Papa looked as if he had gotten into a wrestling match with an ostrich. The chicken gave a loud and meaningful cluck, which Oliver interpreted as "Let go of me, you nincompoop!" Behind him, Oliver heard a set of footsteps coming down the stairs.

"Oh my," Mama said, her mouth wide open as she surveyed the living room. The small coffee table was lying on its side, the couch cushions were askew, and the rug was rippled up in a corner. Feathers were everywhere, and Franz continued to bark from behind the couch.

"It's all under control," Papa told her. The chicken clucked in disagreement.

"Uh-huh," Mama murmured. She blinked, then treated her eyes to a vigorous rub.

"It's not a nightmare," Oliver helpfully told her. "This is really happening."

The doorbell rang, and Franz's howling increased ten notches.

"Now, who could that be?" Mama said, glancing at her watch and then peering out the peephole. It was eight thirty.

Oliver caught a glimpse of the person out the living room window, and his stomach spun upside down. "Don't answer it!" he yelled.

But Mama had already turned the deadbolt and opened the door.

In the doorway was Mr. West and his clipboard.

Twenty-Three

Mr. West looked warily inside, and Franz took the opportunity to jump up on him, knocking his clipboard right out of his hand. Meanwhile, New Dog came trotting down the stairs, followed by Isa, who was saying, "Make way for New Dog! She needs to go to the bathroom!"

Angie, who was standing next to Oliver, volunteered at once. "I'll take her for a walk!" She grabbed New Dog's leash and ran out the back door.

The chicken, sensing Papa's temporary distraction, flapped her wings so aggressively that Papa lost his grip. Going airborne, the chicken headed straight toward Mr. West, who was still standing by the door. The inspector was so focused on retrieving his clipboard and avoiding Franz that he didn't duck and got a face full of chicken feathers. Mr. West blurted out a word that Oliver's parents had forbidden him ever to say, then backed up and tripped on a pile of walking sticks that Laney had been collecting and storing by the door all year long. The chicken was relentless, continuing to peck at Mr. West. Papa and Jessie ran outside to help, and after three attempts, Jessie finally pinned the chicken down with a move that would have made any wrestling coach proud.

Mr. West stood up, holding his clipboard in front of him like a shield.

Mama coughed. "You must be Mr. West. We weren't, uh, expecting you."

"I sent you an email last night saying I was coming at eight thirty a.m.," Mr. West retorted.

"I'm sorry. My kids told me this was rescheduled for Monday," Mama said. "Do you want to come in, or—"

"I am *not* coming in. I have seen all that I need to see." Mr. West scribbled something on his clipboard, ripped off a piece of paper, and handed it to Mama. "I'm *shocked* that you would reschedule the appointment without having addressed any of the many issues I brought up at the last appointment."

"The last appointment?" Mama said slowly.

"I gave the inspection notice to your children. Animals are a violation, and the kitchen needs to be a separate workspace from the rest of the apartment."

"Wait, what? We didn't know about the workspace thing!" Jessie said. The chicken gave a heave against her chest, and Mr. West flinched and backed up two steps.

"Your home processor's license remains revoked," Mr. West said, "and I will be writing a detailed report for your file about my last two visits. You have now two failed inspections and are hereby restricted from having another inspection for one year."

He turned and made his way down 141st Street at a fast clip. The Vanderbeekers watched in silence as his silhouette got smaller and smaller until it disappeared around a corner.

* * *

It was a long time before Mama said a word.

"There was an inspection this past Monday, wasn't there?" Mama asked, turning to the kids.

They nodded.

"And it went badly, didn't it?" Mama asked.

Jessie, who had just released the vagrant chicken into the backyard, swallowed. "He told us the pets were a health hazard. And we thought we could fix it before the next inspection so you didn't have to worry about the *Perch Magazine* photo shoot, but we didn't know about the kitchen needing to be a separate workspace—"

Mama held up a hand. "Have I been operating my business *illegally* this whole week?"

Isa looked at Mama. "Yes. We're so, so sorry."

The Vanderbeekers knew that people showed anger in all sorts of ways. Some people yelled, other people stomped their feet, and some people's faces got red and sweaty. On those rare occasions when Mama got mad, she did not yell or stomp her feet or get red in the face. Instead, she got very, very quiet.

Mama closed her eyes and shook her head. "I just need time . . . to think." She turned around and headed up the stairs to her room. Papa followed Mama, and everyone else followed Papa. When Mama and Papa closed their bedroom door behind them, the Vanderbeeker kids found themselves alone in the hallway.

"I can't believe that happened," Isa whispered, her face pale. "What are we going to do?"

Jessie sighed. "I don't know. He wasn't supposed to come early. We had such a good plan . . ."

Mama's voice drifted through the cracks of her door, and the Vanderbeeker kids leaned in to listen.

"Hi, Nina. It's Maia Vanderbeeker . . . I'm sorry, but I have bad news. We had a run-in with the New York State licensing inspector, and our apartment is not up to code for a home baking business . . . Yes, I figured it would be canceled . . . I'm so sorry . . . Thank you so much for the opportunity . . . Goodbye."

There was a long pause; then they could hear Papa's low voice.

"We'll work this out," he said.

Then Mama's voice. She was so, so quiet that they had to strain to hear her. "Sometimes," she said, "sometimes things are just not meant to be."

* * *

When Mama and Papa opened the door to the bedroom a few minutes later, they found all five kids sitting on the floor. The kids jumped up.

“We’re so sorry,” Isa and Jessie said at the same time.

Laney ran to her mom and hugged her tight. “Are you super mad at us?”

Oliver and Hyacinth couldn’t bear to meet her eyes.

Mama hugged Laney back, then looked at the kids. “You should have told me about the inspection,” she said. “I know you were trying to help, but I could have gotten into huge trouble by operating without a license.”

“We know,” Isa said. “We’re so sorry.”

“Is the photo shoot canceled?” Oliver asked, still not meeting her eyes.

“It is,” Mama said. “My business is officially closed.”

“No!” Hyacinth said. She started to cry.

Mama stroked Hyacinth’s hair. “I’ve never been inspected all these years of operating a business. I should have known pets aren’t allowed, but every time I went online to check on updated regulations, the website was under construction. After a while, I stopped thinking about it.”

“It’s our fault,” Isa said.

“The things that made me fail the inspection are things we can’t fix,” Mama said. “The pets are a part of our lives, and a long time ago we looked at closing the kitchen off. Unfortunately, that type of renovation requires a building permit, which would also mean getting a licensed architect to prepare construction drawings to submit. The waiting list for building permits is long—it could take years. There's nothing to do at this point but acknowledge that this wasn't meant to be and move on."

"But Mama—" Jessie said.

Mama shook her head. "I'll figure something out, but right now Papa and I are going to take a walk. I need to clear my mind. Can you clean up the chicken mess?"

The kids nodded and watched their parents go down the stairs and out the door. And slowly, slowly, they made their way downstairs and began to clean up the living room. If only they could figure out how to clean up the mess they had made of Mama's life.

Twenty-Four

It took nearly two hours to clean the kitchen and living room. When they were done, the apartment would have been an ideal place to have a photo shoot. The floor was free of dust, the kitchen appliances gleamed, and the couch cushions were perfectly fluffed. Oliver even cleaned the bathroom, a chore he had managed to avoid for the last four years. Hyacinth clipped some buttercup winterhazel and a few blooms of forsythia from the backyard and arranged them in a vase on the kitchen island.

The brownstone was officially photo-shoot-worthy, but no magazine photographer would ever capture it.

Jessie looked around at her siblings.

"We need a mood booster," she said. "Let's go to Castleman's."

Everyone brightened for a second before Isa said, "We shouldn't. We need to save up for the flyer fine."

The Vanderbeekers sank back into their dark moods.

"Hey!" Jessie said. "What happened with the recorder?"

Oliver stood up. "Jimmy L had it. He brought it inside . . ." He went to the back door and found the recorder kicked into the corner, probably from when Jimmy L had encountered the chicken chaos that morning. "We need to charge it."

They plugged it in, and when it turned on, they gathered around the device and played it on high speed. It ran for only a few minutes before the screen turned black.

"Darn," Jessie said. "We should have charged it before you used it."

"This stinks," Oliver said.

Laney, tired of the dreariness, got up. "I'm going to introduce Mr. Jeet and Miss Josie to New Dog," she declared. No one responded.

Laney left Paganini behind—she figured having one animal visit at a time was enough for her neighbors—and she coaxed New Dog up the stairs to the second-floor apartment with small dog treats Hyacinth had made the week before. Laney knocked on the door, and Mr. Jeet's home health aide opened it.

"Hi, Miss Laney," Miss Fran said, opening the door and letting her in. Jazz music drifted from the speakers in the living room.

"Hello," Laney said. "I have a new dog to introduce to Mr. Jeet and Miss Josie."

"They're in the bedroom," Miss Fran said. "Go right on in."

Laney led New Dog to the bedroom. The window was open, and Mr. Jeet was awake. He smiled when he saw her.

"Laney!" Miss Josie said. "How nice to see you today. And who is this cutie pie?"

New Dog beelined for Mr. Jeet's bed and rested her head next to Mr. Jeet's hand.

"It's New Dog. She was left in our backyard. We've also gotten chickens, guinea pigs, and kittens."

"Goodness," Miss Josie said. "What are you going to do with them all?"

Laney shrugged. "We tried to find them homes, but it's really hard. And then the health inspector came and said no animals were allowed in the kitchen and he took away Mama's baking license."

"Oh dear," Miss Josie said. "That is terrible news."

"It is," Laney said. "I think New Dog really likes Mr. Jeet."

New Dog had her eyes closed in bliss while Mr. Jeet petted her on the forehead. Mr. Jeet's hands began to slow as he drifted off to sleep, his hand still on her head. New Dog didn't move a muscle, even when Miss Josie and Laney went into the kitchen to have tea and lemon cookies. When they came back, New Dog was in the exact same position as when they had left.

"That is a very nice dog," Miss Fran commented as she straightened up the bedroom.

It was time for Miss Josie to take a rest too, so Laney kissed Mr. Jeet's cheek, kissed Miss Josie's cheek, and hugged Miss Fran before going back downstairs. New

Dog whimpered as they left, casting a look toward the bedroom.

"We'll come back tomorrow," Laney said to New Dog. "Mr. Jeet needs us."

* * *

After the terrible inspection, Isa was too upset to practice. The audition was just a day away, but she had no desire to pick up her violin. Instead, she lay on the couch, staring out the window. Their ground-floor window had the perfect view of people's feet walking by, and she wondered how other people's lives could go on as if it were a completely normal day and not a terrible, no-good, awful day, like it was for them.

The door that led from the first floor to the second opened, and Isa could hear Laney's bouncy footsteps and New Dog's nails tapping on the wood floor. The ground floor opened a few seconds later, and Mama came into the brownstone and went right to the entryway closet, opened it, then began pulling out every item stashed inside. Isa dragged herself from the couch and watched things spill out of the closet: shoes that Hyacinth had outgrown but were still too big for Laney, heavy winter coats that had yet to be packed away, two squishy basketballs, Papa's toolbox, three pairs of galoshes, and an economy package of toilet paper.

"What are you doing?" Isa asked Mama. She and her siblings gathered around the growing mess.

"I'm looking for . . . Ah." Mama pulled out a dusty box that had been in the deepest recesses of the closet and opened the flaps. "Yep, here they are."

"What's going on?" Oliver said with suspicion. He picked up the squishy basketball and attempted to dribble it. It fell to the ground with a sad thud.

"There are my roller skates!" Laney cried, then immediately put them on and hobbled onto the living room carpet.

Isa peeked inside the box Mama had pulled out. It was filled with books, and the book on top was *Accounting Best Practices.*

"Wait, what's going on?" Isa said. "Why do you need these books?"

Mama stood up. "I ran into my old boss just now. You remember Ms. Bachmann, right?"

"Ms. Bachmann?" asked Isa. "Like, Ms. Boring Bachmann?"

"Oh my gosh," Jessie said, her eyes wide. "I completely forgot we called her that."

Mama shoved the toilet paper back into the closet. "She's not that bad."

"Um, yes she is," Jessie said. "Also, she always smelled like medicine. There must be some scientific reason why a person would always smell like medicine."

The last time Isa and Jessie had seen Ms. Bachmann was seven years ago, when they were just six years old, but the memories had stayed with them. Ms. Bachmann had a perpetually pinched forehead, and she had always seemed uneasy when Jessie and Isa came to the office. There was one time when they had a random day off from first grade—a teacher conference or something—and Mama hadn't been able to find a babysitter. She had packed up a bag full of books, art activities, and stickers, dropped then-three-year-old Oliver off at daycare, and brought the twins into the office for the day.

Isa and Jessie quickly grew bored with the activities their mom had packed, and while Mama was on a conference call, the twins explored the office and discovered a box of shiny, brand-new paper clips in the supply closet. They dumped the paper clips out of the box and connected the pieces to make a garland to decorate Mama's bulletin board.

Ms. Bachmann was supposed to be out of the office that day, but when she stopped by unexpectedly to pick up a forgotten file, she discovered the twins in her paper-clip stash.

Two seconds later, Mama was called into Ms. Bachmann's office.

Twenty minutes later, Papa arrived to pick up the kids.

It was one of those childhood memories that Isa remembered as if it had happened yesterday. The scruffy brown carpet, the boring beige walls, the smell of stale coffee, and the whir of the printers as they spat out papers filled with numbers and charts.

Mama grabbed another box and shoved it back into the closet. "It was perfect timing to run into her. I have an interview at her accounting firm on Monday."

"An *interview*? What about your baking?" Isa yelped at the same time Jessie declared, "You can't go back to Ms. Boring Bachmann! We won't let you!" Oliver, Hyacinth, and Laney, who had never met Ms. Bachmann, looked at Mama in horror.

"I can't bake without a home processor's license," Mama told them. "And we need the money."

"Maybe you could use the kitchen at Castleman's Bakery," Isa suggested.

"They don't have space for me," Mama said. "Their kitchen is tiny."

"What about renting a kitchen?" Jessie asked.

Mama shook her head. "We don't have enough money to rent right now. I'm grateful for the accounting opportunity. Who knows? In a couple of years, maybe I'll have saved up enough to rent a commercial kitchen space."

"A couple of *years?*" Hyacinth squeaked.

"Two years seems like a long time, but it really isn't. When you're watching your children grow up, time goes by faster." Mama looked at her oldest kids, seeming to take in their every feature. "Much, much faster."

"But Mama—" Isa protested.

Mama changed the subject. "Isa, how are you

feeling about your audition? I know you're going to be awesome."

Isa didn't respond. Instead, she stared at the stack of accounting books on the ground, wondering how Mama could be so adamant that they follow their own dreams yet be perfectly content not following her own.

Twenty-Five

Mama needed quiet to study for her accounting interview, so she kicked the kids out of the apartment.

"Get some fresh air," she told them.

It was too early to pick up the kittens—Herman had told them not to come until after lunch—so they went upstairs to visit Mr. Beiderman with Franz and New Dog in tow.

Mr. Beiderman opened the door before they even knocked. "You sound like a herd of elephants going up the steps. Is the inspector here? Franz has his leash, right? Remember, I'm only watching them for two hours. Wait, what's *that?*" He pointed a finger at New Dog. Princess Cutie hissed and dashed into the bedroom.

"That's New Dog," Hyacinth told him, walking past him with the two dogs. "She was left outside our door yesterday."

Mr. Beiderman held up a hand. "Hold on a second. Two dogs was not part of the agree—"

"We're not leaving them here," Oliver interrupted, going into the apartment and flopping on the couch. "The inspector already came. Then a chicken attacked him, and he closed Mama's business for the next year. Now she has to be an accountant."

Mr. Beiderman was speechless.

"My stomach hurts," Hyacinth said, sitting down next to Oliver. Franz rested his head on her lap.

"Mine does too. It's a terrible feeling to ruin Mama's dream," Oliver said.

There was a long silence after that, because there was nothing else to say. Even the neighborhood, usually filled with cars honking and buses squealing and dogs barking and people calling out greetings, was oddly quiet.

Finally, Mr. Beiderman spoke. "Our lives are filled with so many moments that make up years and days and hours and seconds. And sometimes when we're going through life, we get to a moment when we lose our way and need help finding it again. You helped me when I was very lost, and I believe you can help your mom find her way too."

Isa was crying. "But what if we can't? What if we screwed things up too much?"

Mr. Beiderman pulled the Vanderbeekers into a rare hug. "The universe is so big, much bigger than you and me and bigger than any of our mistakes. There are always opportunities to forgive and be forgiven. You kids have the power to put so much good and love into this world. I know because you shared that good and love with me."

He gave them one last squeeze and stepped back. "Now I'm going to feed you lunch, and then you're going to get to work."

* * *

After they had eaten, the Vanderbeekers said goodbye to Mr. Beiderman, then left to pick up the kittens from Herman, each thinking about what their neighbor had said. He was certain they could fix things, but to them it seemed impossible. How on earth could they help Mama?

They made their way to Frederick Douglass Boulevard with Franz, New Dog, and their wagon, then turned east on 144th, where Herman's building was. Hyacinth buzzed his apartment number, and Herman's voice came through the intercom.

"Hello?"

"It's Hyacinth," she said into the speaker. "We're here to pick up the kittens."

"Come on up!" The building door buzzed, and the Vanderbeekers stepped inside and got in the elevator to go to the fourth floor. Herman was waiting, his apartment door open.

The Vanderbeekers had been in his apartment only once before, and it was nothing like theirs. First of all, there were no books. In the living room, a big television was mounted on the wall, and there was a white (*white!*) couch with matching armchairs and a glass (*glass!*) coffee table across from it.

Herman led the way down a wide hallway with framed (*framed!*) artwork on the walls, then around a corner. He opened his bedroom door, and they were greeted by an explosion of color. Herman was a master knitter, and most of the things in his bedroom were covered with knitting. Willowy knitted clouds hung from the ceiling among yarn stars threaded with silver. His desk chair was wrapped in navy-blue yarn.

The kittens were batting around little yarn balls, and the gray one was now sporting a tiny red sweater.

"Did you make that sweater?" Hyacinth asked.

"Yeah," Herman said. "And those yarn balls. They love them."

"Cool," Hyacinth said without enthusiasm.

"What's wrong?" Herman asked, looking around at their forlorn faces.

"The inspector came early," Jessie said.

"We weren't ready for him, and then he got attacked by a chicken," Isa said.

"Goodbye, home processor's license," Oliver added.

Herman's eyes widened. "A chicken?"

"Mama has to go back to her accounting job," Jessie added. "A job she hated."

Silence fell over the room, and Hyacinth felt tears pooling in her eyes again.

"Hey!" Herman said. "What's with the doom and gloom?"

The Vanderbeekers looked at Herman warily.

"Your family never lets things get in your way," Herman said. "Remember how you built a garden from scratch? And made friends with the grouchiest person in the neighborhood? Jessie built a water wall. Laney taught a *rabbit* how to do tricks. If you can do all that, you can figure out how to save your mom's business."

"That's what Mr. B said," Oliver said. "But we already tried everything we could think of. We're out of ideas."

"Ideas are everywhere," Herman said.

Laney stood up, Tuxedo the cat in her hands. "I have an idea."

"Awesome," Herman said. "What is it?"

"We're gonna give Mama a bakery!" Laney proclaimed.

"How about we start a little smaller?" Jessie suggested.

"No," Laney said. "I want to start *big*. Really big!"

"And who is going to give her a bakery?" Oliver asked, one eyebrow raised in skepticism.

Laney pointed her index finger at Herman. "He is."

❂ ❂ ❂

Laney wasn't sure why everyone was looking at her with such wide, I-don't-know-what-you're-talking-about eyes. They wanted to help Mama, right?

"That's not— Why do you think—" spluttered Herman.

"Laney, that's silly," Isa said, saving Herman. "Herman can't get Mama a bakery."

Laney kissed Tuxedo on the head. "His dad sells stores, right? *He* can get a place for Mama to start her bakery."

Herman swallowed. "That's my dad, not me. I can't help you."

"Of course you can," Laney said, her eyes full of trust.

Herman was quiet for a moment. The only sound was Franz's dog tags jingling on his collar as he shook off the kittens, who were trying to climb on him.

Then, as if his mind was made up, Herman stood and walked out of the room.

Oliver let out a low whistle. "Now you've done it."

Laney shrugged and gave Tuxedo another kiss. "He's coming back."

Sure enough, Herman came back into the room lugging a laptop and a projector. "Just give me a second to set this thing up." The Vanderbeekers watched as he plugged in cables and pulled the shades over his windows. He pressed a few buttons on his computer, then turned on the projector. The hum of the machine began, and then a spotlight shone on his white wall. An image flickered into view. It was the picture from the promotional postcard, the one of Mr. Huxley standing in front of a fancy building. Along the top it said, "Huxley Realty: Find the Best Home for Your Best Idea."

The Vanderbeekers exchanged looks, then snapped to attention when Herman cleared his throat and flipped to the next slide, which showed a busy Harlem street.

"Harlem is home to thousands of businesses," Herman began, "from top-quality restaurants, clothing establishments, and museums to libraries, banks, coffee shops, and more. It is a thriving economic center, and Huxley Realty can help find the perfect spot for *your* business."

"Wow, you're good at this," Oliver said, impressed.

Herman shrugged. "I've watched my dad give this presentation a bazillion times."

Herman proceeded to flip through a series of slides showing available retail space, which meant places that could be used for businesses like Mama's bakery. Laney wasn't great at calculating really big numbers yet, but she knew that even if she gave up her entire allowance for a very long time, she would not be able to catch up to all the zeroes and commas in that monthly rent number.

Some of the spaces looked really big (bigger than their local library), and some looked tiny (half the size of Harlem Coffee). Some of the places didn't look right for a bakery at all; they were too new and fancy, as if the space belonged to people who wore suits and shiny shoes that rubbed your heels and made blisters.

Herman showed them five properties, throwing out phrases like "recently remodeled," "state-of-the-art technology capabilities," and "short- and long-term leases available." Meanwhile, all the animals dozed off, lulled into a deep slumber by the darkened room and the steady whir of the projector.

"Herman," Jessie interjected, "all these spaces are really fancy. And expensive. How can anyone afford the rent?"

"Well," Herman hedged, "you'd be making money selling the cookies your mom makes. That would pay for the space."

Isa shook her head. "You'd have to sell a thousand cookies every day just to pay rent!"

Herman nodded. "This is New York City. Real estate is expensive." He flipped through the next slides, passing over gleaming glass storefronts and cavernous spaces.

"Wait!" Laney said as Herman's slides flew past. "That one!"

He paused. The slide showed a narrow store. It reminded Laney of the shoe-repair store where Papa had the soles of his work shoes fixed when they got worn down.

"Not that one," Laney said. "The one before."

Herman went back.

Laney was absolutely sure this was the perfect store. "Look at the address!" she said. "It's only a block away!"

Oliver winced. "It looks like a biohazard site."

Jessie agreed. "I would love to get a bacterial sample."

Hyacinth shuddered.

Laney stared at the picture. The awning hung crookedly, and the windows were cracked. A storefront security grate went only a quarter of the way down and was sprayed with graffiti. An interior view showed dusty shelves nailed into the walls, loose wooden boards scattered everywhere, and what looked like four inches of dirt on the ground. When Laney squinted, she could almost imagine it being a cheerful, brightly lit bodega in its glory days. Despite its current decrepit state, Laney knew deep in her heart that this was Mama's bakery.

Herman was skeptical. "This one? Dad only puts this in his presentation to make people want to get the nicer properties."

"So it's not for sale?" Laney asked.

"I mean, I guess someone could lease it," Herman

said. "But no one has ever been interested, because . . ." He gestured to the photo, as if that image held all the reasons in itself.

"What's the rent?" Isa asked. "It's not listed on the slide."

"I've heard Dad try to get some people to rent it, and he says they can have it for free for the first six months but they would have to pay for the renovation costs," Herman said. "It would probably be expensive to fix it up."

At the word "free," the Vanderbeekers' eyes lit up. That was all they needed to hear.

"We'll take it," Laney declared, and the rest of the Vanderbeekers agreed.

Isa handed Oliver her phone. "Call Uncle Arthur. We'll need his help."

The kittens, sensing the excitement in the air, slowly woke from their naps and looked immediately for Franz, who was snoozing under the desk.

But before Oliver could get Uncle Arthur on the phone, they heard the door to Herman's apartment open.

"Herman!" called a deep voice. "Did you see this

wagon in front of our door? It's probably those Leffert kids again. Come out here and put the wagon in front of *their* door. Don't they know we have a rule in this building about leaving stuff in the hallways?"

"Hide!" Herman said to the Vanderbeekers, his eyes filled with panic.

The Vanderbeekers, despite many years' experience with hide-and-seek, discovered that it was not so easy to hide themselves along with five kittens and two dogs in a small bedroom, but they made a valiant effort. Oliver and Laney dropped to the ground and wiggled under the bed, Jessie and Isa squeezed into Herman's closet, and Hyacinth dove under the desk with Franz. Herman snatched up the kittens, put them back into their crate, and shoved the crate behind his beanbag chair, where the kittens protested for two seconds in their tiny kitten voices before growing quiet. New Dog was still sitting in the same place she had been, and Herman left her there, not knowing if she would fuss at being moved.

The door to Herman's bedroom opened. "Herman, did you hear me?"

Herman ran to the door and squeezed out before his

dad could enter. "I'll take the wagon back to the Lefferts' apartment right now," Herman told him. He closed the door behind him, and the Vanderbeekers all breathed a sigh of relief.

Unfortunately, the new dog chose that exact moment to make herself vocally known for the very first time. She opened her mouth, and a clear, high bark echoed throughout the Huxleys' apartment.

Twenty-Six

From her spot in Herman's closet, Isa had a direct view of the bedroom door. Through a tiny opening in the closet, she got a clear look at Mr. Huxley after he burst inside the room. A flash of something went across his face; Isa thought it looked like sadness, or longing, or some other emotion that actually made Isa feel sorry for him.

"Buster?" Mr. Huxley said.

Jessie nudged Isa and mouthed, "Who's Buster?"

Isa raised her hands in an I-don't-know gesture.

"Dad?"

That was Herman, who had just come into view. Mr. Huxley seemed to shake off whatever he was feeling, and his face stiffened back into its normal starchy look.

"What is *that* doing here?" Mr. Huxley asked Herman, pointing at New Dog.

Herman glanced around anxiously, probably to make sure everyone was well hidden, then said, "I found her? On the street?"

Isa and Jessie shook their heads. Herman had broken the cardinal rule of trying to get away with something: responding to a question with a question.

"You *found* this dog?" Mr. Huxley asked. "What do you mean? Does this dog *belong* to anyone?"

"Dad, she—" Herman began.

Mr. Huxley's words steamrolled over Herman. "Does it have a collar? Have you called around to shelters? Did you check if it has a microchip?"

Isa felt Jessie tense next to her, and Isa shook her head. If Jessie burst out of the closet, Herman would only get into more trouble.

"I was going to—" Herman tried again.

"Why does your behavior not surprise me? You

never think before you act! I'm sick and tired of fixing your mistakes!"

Jessie was practically vibrating with frustrated energy at this point, and Isa saw her sister's hand inch to the closet door, when . . .

"Stop it right now!" Hyacinth crawled out from under Herman's desk, and although Isa couldn't see her from her limited view in the closet, she was pretty sure Hyacinth's face was flushed and red, which happened in those rare moments when her sister got upset.

Then there was Laney, crawling out from under the bed. "Yeah, stop being mean to Herman! He's our friend!"

"Oh, for goodness' sake!" Mr. Huxley exclaimed, his arms waving and his voice booming in the small room. "Of course these . . . these . . . *hooligans* are involved!"

A low growl came from under the desk, and gentle, I-wouldn't-hurt-a-fly Franz leaped out in front of Hyacinth and bared his teeth at Mr. Huxley.

"Oh, fudge!" Jessie said, then jumped out of the closet, grabbed Franz's collar, and yanked him back.

Mr. Huxley startled at the sudden appearance of yet another Vanderbeeker.

Isa sighed and emerged as well.

"I don't *think* Franz would bite you," Oliver said to Mr. Huxley, emerging from underneath the bed after Laney. "He's never bitten anyone before, but he sure doesn't seem to like you!"

Mr. Huxley stared at them. "I want all of you out of my apartment right now."

Wordlessly, the Vanderbeekers gathered their stuff. When Oliver walked across the bedroom to pick up the box of kittens behind the beanbag chair, Mr. Huxley's eyes bulged from their sockets. Jessie kept Franz on a short leash just in case, and Hyacinth took New Dog's leash. They filed out of Herman's bedroom, heads held tall. They were not ashamed to be Vanderbeekers, even though Mr. Huxley seemed to find them abhorrent.

Mr. Huxley and Herman followed them out of the apartment, and Isa could hear Mr. Huxley's angry whispers.

"I gave you specific instructions to stay away from that family," Mr. Huxley said.

"I like them," Herman angry-whispered back. "They're my friends."

The Vanderbeekers loaded up the wagon.

"Bye, Herman," Hyacinth said.

"Bye," the rest of the Vanderbeekers echoed.

"I'm sorry," Herman said. "I'll talk to you later."

"He will *not* talk to you later," Mr. Huxley said before closing the door.

They could hear more arguing behind the door, and although Oliver put his ear right up to the front door, he couldn't make out what was being said . . . only the tone, which was not at all friendly.

The Vanderbeekers got into the elevator and exited the building. No one said a word. They went down the street and turned south on Adam Clayton Powell Jr. Boulevard, but instead of continuing down to 141st Street, Laney grabbed Isa's hand and made them turn left on 143rd Street.

"Laney, we have to go home," Isa told her little sister. "The kittens are getting hungry."

"I just need to see something," Laney told her. "Really fast."

Oliver heaved a huge sigh, as if Laney had asked

him to walk five miles in sleet to watch a movie about rabbits and unicorns.

Halfway down 143rd Street, Laney stopped and pointed at a building. "That's it," she told them.

Isa was surprised to see the storefront from Herman's slideshow. "How did you know it was here?"

"The building number was almost the same as Herman's, so I knew it was on the same block on the next street," Laney explained. "Ms. Garcia thinks people use their phones too much, so she taught us how to figure out New York City addresses without technology."

The Vanderbeekers gaped at Laney in astonishment. She was learning a lot more in kindergarten than they thought. The storefront, however, was not so impressive. It was very rundown, even worse than the photo. Laney tried to peek in, but Jessie pulled her back.

"I don't know if your tetanus shot is up-to-date," she told her.

They were silent for a few minutes as they stared at the storefront. A bird chirped from a tree growing through the concrete in front of the store, and ivy crawled up the brick façade on either side of the security gate. It was the kind of storefront you could walk by and never really notice, but to the Vanderbeekers, it seemed to glow and beckon them.

"I'm getting a good feeling from this place," Hyacinth said at last, and Laney beamed in satisfaction.

"Me too," Isa and Jessie said.

"Mr. Huxley is *never* going to let us have it," Oliver pointed out.

"I'll be right back!" Laney said. Then she walked to the store next door—a Jamaican restaurant—and came out with a broom. "I asked the lady if we could borrow a broom, and she said yes." Laney began to sweep the front of the store.

A lady walking a chubby dachshund wearing a big bow around his neck went by. Franz and New Dog perked up and sniffed the dachshund; the dogs pranced around one another and got their leashes tangled.

"What adorable kittens," the woman said, looking inside the box.

"They're up for adoption," Laney said.

"Are you the ones that put up those flyers I saw?"

"We did!" Laney said. "Do you want to adopt one?"

"No, but I took one of the flyers in case I think of anyone who might want to," the woman replied.

"Oh good!" Isa said. "We were trying to find all of the flyers and were just missing one. Apparently it's illegal to put them up. We got fined four hundred twenty-five dollars."

"That's outrageous!" the woman declared. "You should write the city and tell them you're kids and you shouldn't get fined."

"That's a good idea," Jessie said. "Thanks."

The Vanderbeekers went back to looking at the storefront while the woman admired the kittens.

"Isn't there something about this place that makes it feel like home, in a way?" Hyacinth asked her siblings while trying to untangle Franz's leash. "Like, I can picture it as Mama's bakery with a pretty awning and big glass-paned windows. I see her baking inside, and people ordering cakes for their weddings and for birthday parties. We can have café tables where people can hang out and chat."

Isa recognized the faraway look in Hyacinth's eyes:

it was the same one she got when she was dreaming up her next knitting project. Laney was doing a little dance with her broom. Jessie was scrutinizing the store, probably estimating the dimensions and calculating how many tables could fit inside.

"You're a nice family. Good luck with the kittens," the lady with the dachshund said, observing them, "and the fine."

"Thank you!" they said, and they waved as she continued on her walk.

Isa looked at the storefront, and something flashed across the top of the awning. Along the tree branch walked an adult tuxedo cat—it looked as if it could have been the mom of the kitten in their wagon—and it stared at them with large, solemn eyes.

"That looks just like Tuxedo!" Laney exclaimed.

"Oh my gosh," Oliver said, his eyes wide.

"What?" Isa asked him.

Oliver looked at his sisters with a broad, satisfied grin. "The best idea I've ever had in my whole entire life just popped into my brain."

⁂

Oliver looked from the tuxedo cat sunning itself on the tree to his four sisters. The sun glittered overhead, giving the storefront an ethereal glow.

"What's your great idea?" Jessie asked, nudging him. "It's not like the time you suggested we build a big foam pit in the backyard, right?"

Oliver took a breath. "It's an even *better* idea. Angie was telling me about this cat café in Brooklyn that has adoptable cats roaming around—"

Hyacinth interrupted. "We can bring the kittens there!"

"No, I thought—" Oliver began.

"Don't let anyone adopt Tuxedo!" Laney squeaked.

Jessie shook her head. "We really need to get the abandoned animals adopted. We've stressed out Mama enough."

"So my idea—" Oliver began again.

"But I love Tuxedo! We can't give her away!" Laney said.

"Laney, Mama was really clear," Jessie said.

Oliver couldn't take it any longer. "WILL EVERYONE BE QUIET AND LISTEN TO MY GREAT IDEA?"

There was a long silence.

Oliver took a deep, calming breath, just like his fifth-grade teacher had taught his class to do after PE and before math class. "I don't think we should bring our kittens to that café."

"You don't?" Laney asked.

"Nope." Oliver looked out at his siblings and grinned. "I think we should open our own cat café."

Twenty-Seven

It was decided: the Vanderbeekers needed to go to Brooklyn for research.

First they stopped off at home, where they found Mama asleep at the dining room table, her head on her accounting book. They tiptoed around her, dropped off the animals, picked up their MetroCards, and headed out the door toward the subway.

They reached the station and descended underground. After everyone had swiped through the turnstiles, they got onto the number three train to Brooklyn and settled in for a long ride.

Laney didn't know why Oliver disliked the subway so much. She always thought that the longer the subway ride, the better. That day, Laney chose a seat at

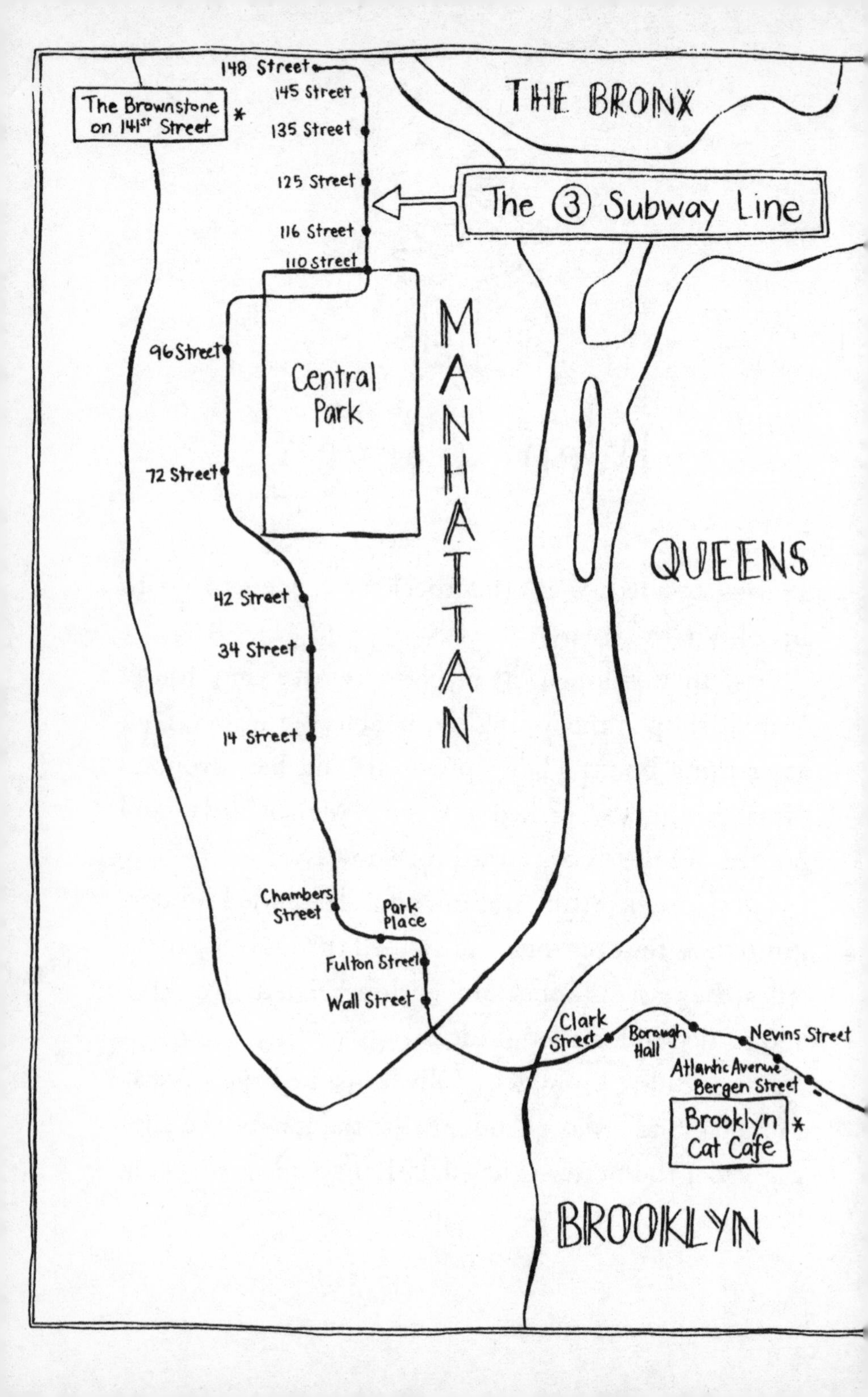
THE BRONX
The Brownstone on 141st Street *
148 Street
145 Street
135 Street
125 Street
The ③ Subway Line
116 Street
110 Street
96 Street
Central Park
72 Street
MANHATTAN
QUEENS
42 Street
34 Street
14 Street
Chambers Street
Park Place
Fulton Street
Wall Street
Clark Street
Borough Hall
Nevins Street
Atlantic Avenue
Bergen Street
Brooklyn Cat Cafe *
BROOKLYN

the end of the group because she liked the possibility of sitting next to a yet-to-be-met friend. It turned out to be Laney's lucky day, because when the train stopped, a man wearing a cape and a tall stovepipe hat entered their car, rolling a large wooden box of balloon animals sticking out in all directions. And of all the empty seats in the whole car, he took the one right next to Laney!

"Hi," Laney said at once. "Did you make all those balloon animals by yourself?"

"I did," he replied. He started poking around his bin, pulling balloons out and piling them on Laney's lap. "Ladybug! Heart wand! Monkey holding a banana! Octopus! Clownfish!"

Laney laughed as the balloon animals overflowed off her lap. Jessie grabbed some of them before they fell to the ground.

"I'll teach you how to make a dog," the man told Laney.

Laney considered their destination. "How about a cat?"

The balloon artist pretended to be put out. "Fine."

Another lucky thing was that he was going to

Brooklyn too. He had to stay on the subway all the way to Rockaway Avenue, which was even farther than their stop. He passed out balloons to riders and taught them how to twist them into cats, and the subway was soon filled with felines of all colors. It made the time fly by, and before they knew it, they had reached their destination and had to say goodbye. Armed with a dozen cat balloons, the Vanderbeekers went in search of the Brooklyn Cat Café.

* * *

The café was everything the Vanderbeekers could ever have hoped for. There was a bit of a line to get inside, and when they finally entered, they found a space with lots of natural light, a display case full of cupcakes, a cappuccino machine, and about ten cats roaming around. There were special climbing shelves built into the walls for the cats, and elaborate trees with hidey holes. On the walls were descriptions of the cats—all rescues up for adoption—including detailed information about their personalities and preferences.

" 'Jeep,' " Hyacinth read out loud from one of the flyers. " 'This three-year-old tabby was found under a

Jeep in Astoria. He is a total love bug and gets along with cats, dogs, adults, and children. He's looking for a forever home with a sunny window spot and lots of love.' "

"We could adopt him," Laney suggested.

"No," said Jessie and Isa.

"We can't go home with *more* cats," Oliver said. "That defeats the purpose!"

"We need to get *our* kittens adopted," Isa said gently.

"Except for Tuxedo," Laney said.

No one responded.

"Can I help you?" A teenager wearing a knit hat, skinny jeans, and a ripped T-shirt that said "Park Slope Cat Café" on the sleeve waved to them from behind the counter.

"Do you have chocolate sea salt caramel cookies?" Oliver asked.

"Nope. Only cupcakes here," the teenager answered.

Oliver frowned while Isa gave the teenager two dollars so they could buy one cupcake to share.

"Are you the owner?" Laney asked.

The teenager laughed. "No, but she's here if you want to meet her."

"We do," Laney said solemnly, then held out a purple cat balloon. "And this is for you."

"Thanks." The girl took the balloon, then turned her head and yelled, "Molly!"

A few seconds later, a woman wearing a dress printed with cats emerged from the back room.

Laney immediately ran to her, gave her a green cat balloon, and unzipped her jacket to show off her unicorn-themed outfit.

"I can already tell we'll be friends," Molly said. "I'm Molly."

Laney introduced everyone, and then Jessie went on to explain why they were there. Molly listened, then put five cupcakes on a plate. "These are on the house. Let's sit down. Do you have a notebook? I have lots of advice."

Jessie pulled out her science notebook from her back jeans pocket and scribbled furiously while Molly spoke about getting sponsors like cat food and litter companies, pairing up with a cat rescue organization, what an ideal café layout would be (a place to prepare food separate from the café area, a place for the cats and customers to interact, and a place for the cats when they need a break from people), and the state permits and licenses they'd need.

"How are cats allowed in a café?" Hyacinth asked. "Mama lost her home processor's license because there were pets in our apartment."

"The kitchen and the customer area must be clearly separated," Molly told them. "The Department of Health is very strict about that. You'll have to submit architectural blueprints to show them that food can be prepared safely without cross contamination."

By the end, Jessie's hand ached from the six pages of notes she had taken.

"I think it's a fabulous idea to open a cat café in Harlem," Molly said. "So many cats languish at the Animal Care Center because no one sees them. If they're in a café, at least they get a fair chance of being seen and eventually adopted."

Oliver had finished his cupcake and was now holding a cat that had taken a liking to him. "It looks like it brings in a lot of business," he said, nodding at the line going out the door.

Molly whistled. "We've been filled to capacity every day since we opened last year. Honestly, I would be happy if you took some business away from me. We can't keep up with the demand."

Since there were customers waiting for a table, the Vanderbeekers thanked Molly, promised to keep in touch, and headed out the door.

"Well?" Oliver said as they left the café and made their way back to the subway. "Did I have the best idea ever or what?"

The Vanderbeekers didn't hesitate for even a millisecond: "Yes!"

Twenty-Eight

The five Vanderbeekers managed to not let one hint about the cat café slip past their lips at dinnertime, and afterward they went into the backyard with Franz, New Dog, and the kittens.

Stretching out on the grass, they watched the animals play. It was eight o'clock, and the chickens had already retreated to their shed to roost. Because Uncle Arthur had finished the treehouse early the day before, he'd had time to install a roosting bar in the shed that sat in the backyard. Jessie had helped him clear out all the old junk, and they spread sawdust on the ground and put some chicken feed, water, and kitchen scraps inside. They also set up wooden apple crates in case these chickens were of the egg-laying variety.

"I've been thinking," Jessie said, "that we need to make a business plan."

"What's a business plan?" Laney asked.

"It's a document that sets out a business's objectives and strategies for achieving them," Jessie said.

"Business objective: to not ruin Mama's life," Oliver suggested.

"Business objective: to create a neighborhood bakery that has the best cookies in the world," Isa said.

"Business objective: to help rescued kitties find forever homes," Hyacinth added.

Jessie wrote everything down except what Oliver had said. "Okay, now we need strategies. Basically everything Molly said this afternoon: Partner with a local animal-rescue organization. Obtain sponsors for cat care. Get licenses from the Department of Health. Create a website. Raise money for renovations. Bake Uncle Arthur lots of muffins in exchange for help with the renovations. Ask Allegra to design a logo. Create a menu."

"Ooh, we can put cat-puccinos on the menu!" Hyacinth said. "And serve them in a cat mug!"

"For the cats?" Oliver asked, puzzled.

"No, for the customers," Hyacinth explained. "And we can make cupcakes and call them cat-cakes!"

"*Those* are for the cats, right?" Oliver said.

Hyacinth huffed. "Oliver, of course not! It will be a cat-cake because Mama can put a cat footprint in the frosting."

"Not a *real* cat footprint, right?" Oliver asked. He imagined holding up a kitten and pressing her paw into the frosting. "That doesn't sound so sanitary."

Hyacinth didn't bother to respond.

"Just make sure Mama has chocolate sea salt caramel cookies on the menu," Oliver said, pointing at Jessie's document. "Write that down."

"I think a well-researched plan will make a big difference," Jessie said, pretending Oliver hadn't spoken. "Mr. Huxley is a businessman; he won't put personal feelings ahead of making money. Herman said his dad makes three percent of the lease amount as long as Mama keeps renting the space from him."

"You write the business plan," Oliver told Jessie as he stood up and brushed the grass from his pajama pants. "I'll do another night of surveillance. We still need to find out who's leaving these animals!" He went inside the brownstone to grab supplies, then made his way up the ladder and into his treehouse. A moment later, his flashlight flickered on and the treehouse glowed with warmth.

Hyacinth replayed the day in her mind: the arrival of the chickens, the disastrous inspection, and the trip to Brooklyn. Something else had happened that day that could help with the cat café idea, but the thought was elusive and ran away every time she was close to touching it. Hyacinth lay down in the grass and stared at the clear sky, hoping the cosmos would help her remember. Stars were a rarity due to New York City's light pollution, but after a few minutes of looking into the inky night, a star emerged! Hyacinth remembered the nursery rhyme about wishing on the first star, so she closed her eyes, made a wish, and breathed it out into the universe.

❋ ❋ ❋

In the treehouse, Oliver was more prepared for the second night's reconnaissance. He had brought up an extra blanket earlier that day to make sleeping on the wood-plank floors more bearable, and he plugged the video camera into the long power cord that Jessie had set up for him. No way would the battery run out on him tonight.

Oliver flicked his flashlight on and scanned the treehouse bookshelves for something to read. He wasn't in the mood for anything suspenseful or new; he wanted a story where he knew everything would turn out all right. He scanned the titles, and his eyes landed on that familiar beige spine with the block-print type. It was exactly the story he wanted, and he pulled it from the shelf, settled into his sleeping bag, and began to read.

Once there were four children whose names were Peter, Susan, Edmund, and Lucy.

The comforting words, which had been read to him at least a dozen times, relaxed him so much that he was asleep before he finished the first page.

* * *

With all that had happened that week, Isa had had much less practice time than anticipated. To make matters worse, the incident at the Huxleys' apartment had unmuted New Dog's voice. She barked hysterically anytime Isa practiced her violin that day.

Jessie was hunched over the computer, typing out the business plan, when Hyacinth entered the room. Isa was reading the flyer-violation email from the City of New York on her phone.

"This is a disaster," Isa said. "I don't know how to respond."

"Oh, I can help you. Apologizing is easy," Hyacinth said.

Isa raised an eyebrow.

The second Jessie got off the computer, Hyacinth pointed to the desk chair. "Isa, sit down and I'll tell you what to write. All you have to do is imitate the best apologizer ever: Anne Shirley from *Anne of Green Gables.*"

To: The City of New York

From: Isa Vanderbeeker

Subject: Re: Violation of §10-119 of New York City's Administrative Code

To Whom It May Concern:

It was with great sorrow that we received your email dated April 3 regarding the fine we incurred for putting up flyers about pet adoption in Harlem. When we received the attached notice about the fine, we were devastated, not only because we cannot afford to pay you $450 but because we are law-abiding citizens and would never want to break a city administrative code. We are just kids, and we did not know any better. Now that we are well informed about that law, we will certainly follow it. If you can find it in your heart to forgive us (and also not charge us $450), we would be forever grateful.

Sincerely,

Isa Vanderbeeker, age 13
Jessie Vanderbeeker, age 13
Oliver Vanderbeeker, age 10
Hyacinth Vanderbeeker, age 8
Laney Vanderbeeker, age 6

Hyacinth, satisfied that she had captured the spirit of Anne, said good night to Isa and went back to her bedroom. After rereading it three times to check spelling and grammar, Isa pressed send and swiveled in her desk chair to tell Jessie. Her sister was already asleep, New Dog curled in a tight ball at her feet.

Isa tiptoed past them, hoping New Dog wouldn't

wake up. She really needed to practice and didn't want New Dog to start barking again. On the way to the basement, she passed Mama, who was sitting at the dining room table with her accounting books.

"Practicing again?" Mama inquired.

Isa nodded. "Mr. Van Hooten is going to call in half an hour to hear me play."

"Good luck."

"Thanks," Isa replied. She kissed her mom's cheek, then headed downstairs.

In the basement, Isa pulled out her battered and marked-up sheet music and reviewed it one more time. She had analyzed each inch of this music for the past four months, and she didn't want to give the judges any excuse not to accept her. A few measures from the end of the piece, her phone chimed with an incoming video-chat request. She clicked it, and Mr. Van Hooten's face appeared on the screen.

"Hi!" he boomed. "How are you feeling about tomorrow?"

Isa hurriedly pressed the button that decreased the volume. "I don't know," she told him. "I'm worried."

"Ah, why worry? You will be brilliant."

"How is Amsterdam?" she asked, changing the subject. Mr. Van Hooten had gotten married last year, and he and his spouse were celebrating their one-year anniversary in Amsterdam, the capital of the Netherlands.

"It is a beautiful city!" He turned his phone around and aimed it out the window. Isa could see the glow of streetlamps and the faint outlines of buildings.

"It's too dark," Mr. Van Hooten said. "I'll send you a picture tomorrow morning. You will fall in love with this place. One day you will come here and play music at the Royal Concertgebouw."

"Maybe," Isa said, her stomach flipping at the thought of a huge concert hall in a foreign country. "But I'm nervous auditioning just for a high school orchestra."

"You will be brilliant," Mr. Van Hooten repeated. "Let me hear your piece, and then I must go to bed. It's midnight here."

Isa winced. "I forgot about the time change! I'm so sorry!"

Mr. Van Hooten shook his head. "We were at a concert. We got home only thirty minutes ago."

Isa smiled, relieved he hadn't stayed up to hear her, and lifted her violin to rest on her shoulder. She took a deep breath and began to play.

Sometimes when Isa played, the vibrations of the violin filled her heart with energy and love. Sometimes the notes shimmered in the air and floated to the ground as if they were fireworks drifting lazily in the breeze after they exploded.

Tonight, however, the notes didn't shimmer. Each note dropped to the ground and shattered, and Isa knew halfway through that Mr. Van Hooten would be disappointed.

When she played the last note, she put down her violin before the string had even finished vibrating. "I'm sorry, Mr. Van Hooten," she began. "I've been working so hard, but—"

"Isa," Mr. Van Hooten interrupted, "you need rest. Something is on your mind, yes?"

Isa's mind *was* full of everything that had happened that week: of home license inspectors and homeless kittens and flapping chickens, of guinea pigs and a dog with a scar on her nose, of Mama's ruined business and a dilapidated storefront. She looked at Mr. Van Hooten on the screen, and as usual, he seemed to know what was on her mind without her saying a word.

"Things always get better," he said. "You've put in the work. Your fingers and your body know the music. Now you need to let your heart know it too. Do your best, and remember the important things—"

But before he could finish the sentence, the connection between them failed. Isa stared at the phone, willing for Mr. Van Hooten to appear again and tell her what exactly it was that she should remember. But the screen stayed blank.

Isa waited for a few more minutes before putting down her phone and picking up her violin. If she got the piece *exactly* right, maybe somehow everything else in her life would fall into place as well.

APRIL

MONDAY	TUESDAY	WEDNESDAY
1	2	3
	Find homes for kittens!	Find homes for kittens and guinea pigs!
←	S·	P·R·I·N·G

Friday, April 5

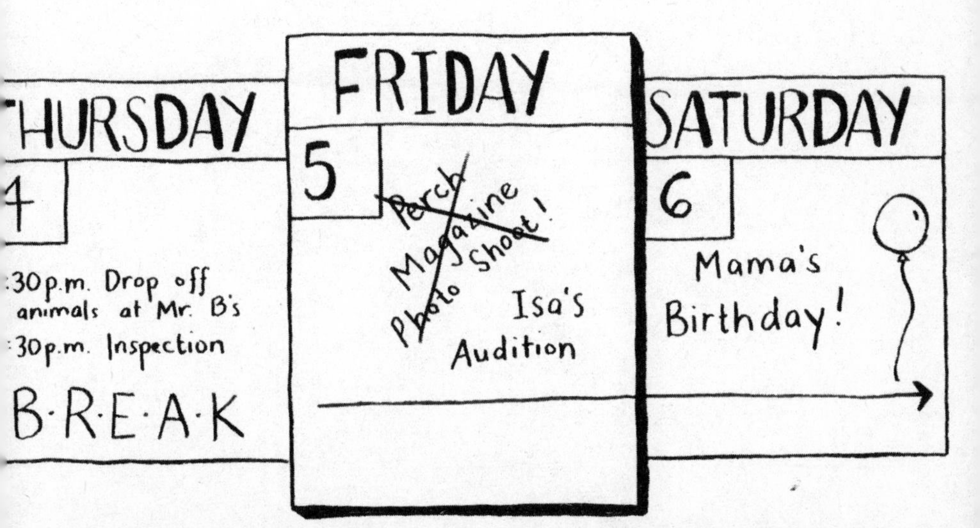

Twenty-Nine

The next morning, Hyacinth woke up and shivered. She glanced at the thermometer outside her window. Jessie had installed one outside everyone's bedroom window the previous Christmas. The temperature had dropped twenty degrees overnight.

Hyacinth pulled her blanket around her, stuffed her feet into slippers, and checked on the animals. The guinea pigs were buried under a pile of shredded newspaper, and the kittens were sleeping in a pile in the corner of the crate. Satisfied that they weren't cold, she headed out of the bedroom with Franz following her sleepily. As she went down the stairs, she tried to remember her strange dream from the night before. It had to do with Mr. Huxley, she knew, but after that, things went hazy.

Downstairs, she expected to see Papa, who was an early riser, but instead Hyacinth found Mama under a throw blanket on the couch with a book as thick as Hyacinth's encyclopedia of knitting stitches, which was so heavy she never moved it from its spot on top of her desk.

Hyacinth crawled under the blanket next to Mama, trying to absorb some of her warmth. The book was open to a page that said "U.S. GAAP Rules."

"What does that mean?" Hyacinth asked.

Mama took off her glasses and rubbed her temples. "It's something I need to *re*-remember for my accounting interview."

Hyacinth eyed the book with skepticism. "That looks complicated. Are all the pages in that book like that?"

"Sort of," Mama said. "Accountants have to be very smart."

"You're smart," Hyacinth said.

"Thank you," Mama said. She kissed Hyacinth on the cheek, then went back to her reading.

"Mama?" Hyacinth asked.

"Mmm-hmm?"

"I'm sorry we ruined your business."

Mama cupped Hyacinth's face in her hands and kissed her nose. "You know what? The inspector would have closed my business anyway. It's not your fault."

Hyacinth was not reassured.

"Hey," Mama said, catching a tear from Hyacinth's cheek with her thumb. "I think we both need some cheering up. Let's make sugar cookies."

For the next hour, Hyacinth and Mama settled into the familiar rhythm of mixing butter, sugar, flour, baking soda, eggs, and a pinch of salt. After they let the dough chill briefly in the freezer, Hyacinth watched her mom's strong arms roll it out; then Hyacinth pressed her cat-cookie cutter into the sheets. Mama deftly transferred Hyacinth's cutouts to a baking tray and slid it into the oven.

An hour later, the rest of the Vanderbeekers, except Oliver, who was sleeping outside in the treehouse, awoke to the brownstone's happy creaks and the comforting smell of sugar cookies. The heat from the oven spread warmth throughout the apartment, and the one thought that drifted over the Vanderbeeker kids as they awoke was that they absolutely could not let Mama down this time.

They needed to get her that bakery.

❊ ❊ ❊

Oliver did not wake up to the sounds of Mama and Hyacinth giggling or the sweet smell of sugar cookies. He woke up to the clucking of chickens and the blare of a car horn. He sat up and cupped his hands over his face, blowing warm air to defrost his nose. Pulling his hoodie over his head, he sat up to look out the window. The chickens were awake and pecking the ground, but there didn't seem to be any additional animals.

Oliver checked the camcorder—it was still running—and he switched it off and unplugged it from the extension cord. Then he slipped the device into his hoodie pocket and slid down the climbing rope. The chickens gathered around him, having recognized him as the source of their meals. Oliver promised to feed them after he ate his own breakfast, and he left the hungry chickens pecking at the door in protest when he slipped inside the brownstone.

Once inside, he basked in the warmth of the kitchen and the smell of sugar cookies. His favorite smell in the whole world was chocolate sea salt caramel cookies, but sugar cookies were definitely in his top ten. Mama and Hyacinth wore matching aprons; Hyacinth had flour on her nose. Franz was weaving between their legs, sniffing out a trail that would hopefully lead to a stockpile of dropped cookie dough.

"Any more animals?" asked Jessie, who was standing by the kitchen island, crunching on an apple.

Oliver shook his head. "And the recorder actually worked last night too."

"Darn," Laney said.

"I know," Oliver agreed. "What a waste."

"I was hoping for a hedgehog," Laney grumbled. "Or a mini-pig."

"Those are illegal in New York City," Jessie told her.

Laney scowled at the injustice. Then she shoved a big bite of buttermilk pancakes into her mouth.

Oliver's stomach rumbled, and he reached out for a plate, but Mama swatted his hand away.

"Wash your hands first," she said, going to the kitchen sink and gesturing him over. "Since apparently we are operating a farm now."

Oliver went to the sink, and Mama took the soap dispenser and pumped a healthy glob of soap onto his hands. He got the suds going, then let the warm water bring feeling back into his cold fingers. After he ate breakfast, he climbed into the shower and let the hot water warm the rest of his body up. Once he was dry and in clean clothes, he headed downstairs to see if he could find the sugar cookies. The doorbell rang when he was halfway down, and there was the usual mad rush—Franz howling, New Dog barking, the kittens scrambling to see what the commotion was, George Washington fleeing up the stairs to hide from the intruders. Oliver opened the door to find Benjamin Castleman.

"Hey," Benjamin said.

"Hey," Oliver said. "Nice jersey."

Benjamin looked down at his shirt, then back at Oliver. "Thanks. Is Isa home?"

"I'm coming, I'm coming!" Isa said, flying down the stairs, her hair streaming down her back. "I just need to get my violin!" She was wearing a black dress and no shoes.

"Wow," said Benny.

"Right?" Oliver said. "She's all stressed about this audition. Hey, want to play basketball with Angie and me later?"

"I've never seen her in that dress before," Benjamin said.

Oliver wrinkled his nose, sensing that Benjamin's attentions were focused elsewhere, and left him at the door to return to his original purpose for coming downstairs: sugar cookies.

A few moments later, Isa emerged from the basement with her violin.

"I thought your audition wasn't until ten thirty," Mama said, looking at her watch.

"I want to get there early so I can warm up," Isa explained.

By that time, the rest of the family had gathered in the living room to wish Isa luck and give her hugs. Hyacinth and Laney kept touching her lace dress and commenting on how pretty it was. Benjamin didn't utter a word, but Oliver could tell he agreed. Jessie handed Isa a pair of black shoes. Mama gave her a kiss and said she was proud of her. Papa gave Isa his usual game-day pep talk about playing hard and how the greatest glory was giving it your all, something he had probably borrowed from his high school basketball coach, then handed her a coat, since it had turned so cold overnight. Oliver sat down on the couch with his cookies and watched everyone say goodbye as if Isa were leaving them for three decades instead of three hours.

After the long goodbye, Papa went to work and Mama curled up on the couch, glasses on, the *Accounting Best Practices* book in her lap. Oliver, hoping Jessie wouldn't remember that she had volunteered him to help finalize the business plan, grabbed another cookie and went to the backyard. The chickens ran to him, their wings flapping.

"Okay, okay," Oliver said to them, trying not to step on any chickens as he made his way to the feed bin. It was difficult to avoid them, harder than it had been the day before. Why was that?

Then Oliver stopped and counted the chickens.

One.

Two.

Three.

Four.

Five.

Six.

Seven.

Seven chickens!

* * *

Jessie was in her room at the computer, adding the finishing touches to the business plan, when Oliver burst into her bedroom.

"There are seven chickens outside," Oliver blurted out. "*Seven!*"

"What?" Jessie said. She was trying to complete a thought she had just had about business outcomes.

"*Seven* chickens!" Oliver said. "We need to look at the video! Hyacinth! Laney!"

Hyacinth and Laney rushed into the room.

"What's going on?" Hyacinth said. "Is everyone okay?"

Oliver was punching buttons on the recorder. "There were three more chickens in the backyard this morning. I didn't notice until I was feeding them. If someone left them there, they should have been caught on camera."

Jessie grabbed the recorder from Oliver. "Don't randomly press buttons! You're going to accidentally delete it!" She tinkered with it, then held it out so everyone could see the video play on the tiny recorder.

"Gosh, that screen is so tiny," Laney said.

Jessie set the video playback at ten times the normal speed, yet the recorder showed the same view of their back door, dimly lit with a single porch light. Ten minutes later, they had reviewed nearly three-quarters of the video.

"Maybe the chickens heard that the Vanderbeeker backyard was the place to be, and they flew over the fence," Jessie said.

"Or the camera is angled wrong," Oliver said gloomily. "Maybe the person opened the gate, snuck the chickens inside the backyard, then left again without crossing the back door."

A morning light began to creep into the footage—the sun was rising—and Jessie's arm was tired of holding the camera. "I don't think we're going to find any—"

"Wait! There!" Laney shouted at the same time Hyacinth yelled, "I see something!"

Jessie paused the video, rewound a little bit, then played it again at the regular speed. The shadow of a person crossed in front of the door, then disappeared. Three chickens ran across the screen.

"I can't believe it," Jessie said.

Oliver glanced at Jessie. "Maybe we should look at the video again." He reached out to take the recorder.

"We don't need to see it again," Jessie said, snatching the recorder back. "We *all* know who that is."

Thirty

A few minutes later, Jessie, Oliver, Hyacinth, and Laney were knocking on Miss Josie and Mr. Jeet's door.

Miss Josie opened the door and looked around. "No animals today?"

"They're resting," Laney told her.

"Sorry to bother you," Jessie said, "but do you know if Orlando is around this week?"

"I can't imagine why not," Miss Josie said. "He called yesterday to check on me."

"Do you know where he lives?" Jessie asked. Even though Jessie and Orlando had hung out nearly every day since he had moved to Harlem nine months earlier, she had not once been to his apartment, a fact she now suddenly found suspicious.

"I haven't been to his place in months—I barely leave the apartment these days unless I'm taking Mr. Jeet to the doctor—but he lives in the white brick building on 122nd Street between Adam Clayton Powell and Frederick Douglass. North side of the street, sort of near the middle. He lives on the second floor, apartment 2A. I don't remember the building number."

"We'll find it," Jessie said.

"Thanks, Miss Josie," Laney said, giving her a hug.

"I hope everything is okay," Miss Josie said, her face creased with worry.

"Me too," Laney said, glancing at Jessie, who looked as mad as the time Laney had (accidentally) sat on her experiment and ruined three weeks' worth of scientific research.

"Tell him he should come over for dinner tomorrow," Miss Josie said.

"Will do," Jessie said before turning Laney's shoulders toward the staircase and nudging her downstairs.

"Where are we going now?" Laney asked.

"Orlando's place," Jessie said.

Jessie popped her head inside their apartment to let Mama know they were taking a walk.

"Put jackets on," Mama asked. "And take the dogs with you, please!"

Franz was dozing in a patch of sun, but New Dog was pacing back and forth and whining.

Jessie let out an impatient sigh, but she grabbed jackets while Hyacinth and Oliver leashed the dogs up. Before long, they were walking down Frederick Douglass Boulevard, passing sandwich boards advertising hair braiders and southern fried chicken. They walked south all the way down to 122nd Street, then made a left.

"Hey, this is the same block as the animal shelter," Hyacinth said.

"Isn't it weird that we've never been to Orlando's place?" Oliver asked. "He practically lives at our brownstone."

"It *is* weird," Jessie said, her voice clipped.

"Are you mad at him?" Laney asked.

"You bet I'm mad at him," Jessie said, her arms crossed. "He lied about being out of town this week when we were supposed to be working on our science fair project, and now we find out that *he's* the one who's been leaving all those animals at our home? Nope. Not cool."

"Maybe he has a good reason," Hyacinth said, jogging a little to keep up with Jessie's long, indignant strides.

Jessie didn't respond, and it made Laney really, *really* hope that Orlando had a good reason, because Jessie did *not* seem in the mood for anything less than the best excuse in the world.

❋ ❋ ❋

The Vanderbeekers followed Miss Josie's directions to Orlando's apartment. They were searching for the white building when they saw Orlando's familiar silhouette rambling toward them from the opposite end of the street. Laney immediately broke into a run to greet him, and by the time the rest of the Vanderbeekers caught up with her, she was talking a mile a minute. Franz let out an I've-missed-you-so-much howl, and New Dog licked Orlando's hand.

"Was that really you, Orlando, who left all of those

animals at our place?" Laney was saying. "Why would you do that? And did you know that Mama's baking business got closed down? Mama has to go back to her accounting job, which no one wants her to do. And Jessie is super-*duper* mad at you because you were supposed to be doing your science fair project with her this week but you said you were out of town and you weren't."

Jessie crossed her arms and stared at Orlando. His shirt was dirty, his pants had holes in the knees, and his eyes had dark circles under them.

"Wait, what happened to your mom's business?" Orlando asked.

"It was closed down," Oliver told him. "Health violations because of the animals."

Orlando ran his hands through his hair and looked away from the Vanderbeekers. "Oh no. What did I do?"

"It's okay," Hyacinth said, patting his arm. "It wasn't your fault."

Jessie glared at her siblings. "What do you mean, it's not his fault?" Then she looked back at Orlando and pointed a finger at his chest. "You ruined Mama's inspection. Her business was destroyed because of those animals!"

"I'm so sorry, Jessie. I didn't know—"

"And why did you tell me you were out of town?" Jessie interrogated. "You lied to me."

"Jessie, chill," Oliver said.

"I will *not* chill!" Jessie yelled.

"I will make it up to you, I promise," Orlando said, his eyes pleading. "Let me explain."

Everyone looked at Jessie, and she finally huffed and said, "Fine. But this better be good."

After breathing a sigh of relief, Orlando said, "Come with me." He turned around, and they followed him down the street until he stopped at the end of the block, where there was an abandoned parking lot filled with broken bottles and trash.

"Well, that's gross," Jessie said. "*This* is what you wanted to show us?"

Orlando ignored her. "Did you know this lot is where the most animals are abandoned in the whole entire city?"

"Why?" Hyacinth asked.

Orlando pointed across the street. "Because

Manhattan's Animal Care Center is right there, and when someone needs to give up their pet, that's where they go. But sometimes the owners don't want to go inside and fill out paperwork or pay the owner-surrender fee, so they leave the animals chained to this fence and hope the shelter employees see them and bring them inside."

Jessie softened. The Animal Care Center was not great, but being abandoned in a dirty lot was much, much worse.

"Sometimes they get brought inside and processed for adoption," Orlando said, "but there's not enough space for all the animals that are getting abandoned, so the animals left out here are usually euthanized right away. I was tired of walking by this lot and seeing the animals here. And since I couldn't take them home, I thought maybe your family could."

"Why didn't you call me instead of leaving them outside our door?" Jessie asked.

There was a long pause.

"Because I felt like I ask you for too much already," Orlando finally said. "I eat at your house all the time. Your dad pays me to help him do chores, even though

I know he doesn't need help. Your mom bought me these shoes! But I couldn't let those animals stay outside like that. I knew you would take care of them."

"Well, Mama definitely did not pay full price for those shoes," Jessie told him, pointing at his sneakers.

"Yeah, she bought me these shoes from the bargain bin when I was six years old," Oliver piped in, pointing at his own sneakers. "It took four years for me to grow into them. Anyway, if we didn't like hanging out with you, we wouldn't let you eat dinner with us."

"That's true," Hyacinth said. "Oliver used to hate Herman Huxley, and you should have seen how mean he was to him."

"We like having you around," Jessie told Orlando. "And you help me with science all the time. I like being science partners with you. It's not like we're tallying up friendship scorecards or anything."

Orlando looked away and coughed, and Jessie thought a mood lightener might be in order. "What's the deal with the chickens, Orlando?"

Her words worked, because he choked out a laugh. "There's a poultry processing plant not too far from here," he told them. "Sometimes the chickens escape."

"And you thought they would be good in our back-yard . . . why?" Jessie asked.

"I don't know," Orlando said. "They looked so lonely wandering around. I was worried they would get run over by a car or that someone would make them into dinner."

"I'm never eating chicken again," Laney declared.

"I like having the chickens in our backyard," Hyacinth said. "They peck at my sneakers."

"We hope they lay eggs," Jessie said. "We gave them nesting cubes."

Orlando finally noticed New Dog and patted her head. Franz, jealous that he had to compete for head rubs with New Dog, pushed his nose into Orlando's hand. "This girl was being bullied by an off-leash dog when I first saw her," Orlando told them. "I couldn't let her stay chained to the fence."

"I'm glad you saved her," Laney told him.

"We'll find her a home," Orlando said. "Right, buster?"

Hyacinth froze. Where had she heard that name before? Then she remembered.

Mr. Huxley!

"Buster! That's it!" Hyacinth yelled. "We need to get Isa, now!" She sprinted down the street with both dogs chasing her.

"Hyacinth!" Oliver called as he ran to catch up.

"We need to get Isa! Then we're going to convince Mr. Huxley to give us that storefront!" Hyacinth yelled back.

And just like that, the Vanderbeekers, plus Orlando, Franz, and New Dog, were off again, running full speed toward Isa and her audition.

Thirty-One

It was unfortunate that when Isa got nervous, her palms got really sweaty. Sweaty palms did not go well with violin playing.

The audition was running behind, and Isa was sitting in what looked like a kindergarten classroom while she waited for her name to be called. In the room with her were a flutist who was obsessively playing three notes over and over again and another violinist practicing with his mother. The mom was scowling and correcting his posture, and Isa felt a little sorry for him. There was also a cellist, but he wasn't practicing. He was playing a video game on his phone.

Her scheduled audition time had been twenty minutes ago, and she had a feeling she might be next.

Benny hadn't been able to stay—he had a shift at the bakery—and she had been sitting in a too-small chair by herself for forty-five minutes. Isa wiped her sweaty palms on a cloth she kept in her violin case. The door to the classroom opened, and everyone's heads swiveled toward it. A woman wearing her hair in a ponytail and carrying a clipboard stuck her head inside.

"Isa Vanderbeeker?" she said.

"That's me," Isa said.

"You're next."

Isa wiped her palms on the cloth one more time, then grabbed the neck of her violin, hooked the bow on her finger, slung her violin case over her shoulder, and made her way out the door and down a long, dark hallway. Her shoes echoed on the cold linoleum behind the other woman. She began to hear music as they approached the end of the hall, and when they turned the corner, the sound grew louder. The woman with the clipboard stopped in front of a door.

"Wait here," she told Isa, then disappeared around the corner, giving Isa no further instructions.

Isa waited, and a few minutes later, the music stopped. There were some rumblings of conversation, and then the door opened. A boy about her age with hair that looked as if he hadn't combed it in two weeks stepped out of the room. He flashed her a smile, held the door open for her, and said "Good luck" as she passed him.

"Come on in," said a rumbly voice that she would have recognized anywhere. It was Mr. Rochester—the very Mr. Rochester the Vanderbeekers had deceived a year and a half earlier when they had pointed him in the wrong direction when he had had an appointment to see and possibly rent their beloved apartment. He was sitting with two other people: a young woman with curly red hair wearing her coat and a scarf *and* a hat *and* gloves, and an older man. A cane hung from the armrest of the older man's chair. They sat behind tables that faced away from the windows.

"Sorry it's so cold in here," Mr. Rochester said without looking up from the notes he was making on a piece of paper. "This room smelled like rotten food, and we need the windows open to make it bearable."

"We hope it's not too cold for you." The woman shivered as she wrapped her hands around a mug.

"Isa Vanderbeeker, right?" Mr. Rochester asked, finally looking up at her.

Isa swallowed and nodded.

Mr. Rochester glanced at her over the top of his glasses. "Have we met before?"

Isa tried to croak out an answer, but before she could, the woman said, "We're running twenty minutes late. You may begin."

Isa was tempted to wipe her palms on her dress, but she didn't. First, because it was not professional to wipe your hands on your dress in front of judges, and second, because the dress belonged to Allegra, who probably did not want Isa's sweaty handprints on it. Instead, Isa picked up her violin, closed her eyes for a brief second, and took a deep breath.

The Violin Concerto in B Minor, third movement, by Camille Saint-Saëns, begins dramatically. Isa closed her eyes, and she let the image of a crashing storm pummeling the city appear in her mind. She let the piece retreat and grow, remembering Mr. Van Hooten's advice to really linger on the notes and not worry about what was coming up later in the piece.

By the time she had reached the second half, the tempo increased to rapid marcato notes that bounced on the strings. Isa relished the opportunity to play without New Dog barking, without thumps from Laney's gymnastics above her, without interruptions from her siblings.

She approached the climax of the piece, her fingers moving so quickly that her brain didn't seem to register what her body was doing. Then something that was not her violin's music nudged its way into her ears. At first it was a low buzzing, and Isa pushed it away. But the noise only grew louder, until she could ignore it no longer.

She knew that noise. Isa glanced up from her instrument for one fatal moment.

In the window was New Dog, her front paws resting on the windowsill, her head tilted to the sky, barking along with Isa's violin. Franz was too short to see, but she knew he was there because his howls came through the window loud and clear. Jessie and Orlando were collectively trying to pull New Dog away from the window while Hyacinth did the same with Franz. Isa could glimpse the top of Oliver's head as he (unsuccessfully) hid behind a bush, and Laney was jumping up and down and waving at Isa as if they had been separated for months.

Isa's usual demeanor was steady, calm, and able, but

those particular characteristics eluded her at the moment. She was like a violin string wound too tight, ready to snap.

And snap she did, because before she knew it, she burst into big, chest-heaving laughter. The following week, when Isa had had time to process it all, she would blame her reaction entirely on the stress and pressure of the previous five days. She continued to the very last note despite her mini-breakdown. Mr. Van Hooten had trained her to complete auditions even if there was a wardrobe malfunction, a missing accompanist, or, apparently, dogs barking maniacally at her. In the end, it probably didn't matter. The judges weren't paying attention; they were standing at the window.

The older man was lecturing her siblings, pointing his cane at them and talking loudly to make himself heard over the raucous barking.

"This is *quite* unprofessional," the woman said, glancing at her watch.

Mr. Rochester didn't say anything, but when he turned back to look at Isa, she saw that he had placed his memory of her. He absolutely knew they were the family that had sabotaged his apartment hunting less than two years ago. And just like that, Isa's laughter fizzled to flatness.

"Thank you for coming in," he told Isa, sitting back down to fill out his audition notes. "We'll be in touch."

Isa bit her lip and turned to the door. When she opened it, the flutist was standing there, chewing at her pinky fingernail.

"Good luck," Isa told her.

Isa made it only a few steps away from the door when all her siblings, plus Orlando and the dogs, came crashing down the corridor.

"Oh my gosh, Isa, I'm so sorry," Jessie said, breathless.

"Did we mess up your audition?" Hyacinth asked, worried. "I don't know what got into New Dog."

"Of course we messed up her audition. Or at least, *she* did," Oliver said, pointing at New Dog.

New Dog whimpered and let her legs slide on the linoleum until she flattened herself against the floor.

"She runs really fast," Laney added.

"She probably smelled Isa," Orlando told Oliver. "Dog noses have three hundred million olfactory receptors."

"Well, she *could* have heard her," Jessie said. "Dogs can hear four times the distance of a human with normal hearing. And you know how much she loves Isa's violin."

"We're sorry," Hyacinth said to Isa. "Really, really sorry."

Isa looked back at them. They did look very apologetic, especially the two dogs. Her mind flashed back to what Mr. Van Hooten had said the day before, right before their connection was cut off: *Do your best, and remember the important things.*

"It's okay," Isa said. "I forgive you."

"Good," Oliver said. "Because we need your help."

* * *

As they speed-walked to Herman's apartment, Hyacinth did her best to explain her idea.

"Remember when we were hiding at Herman's place and his dad came in? And remember how he looked at New Dog and called her Buster?"

"Yeah," Isa said.

"It was bugging me," Hyacinth said, "and this morning it struck me: New Dog must remind him of a childhood dog or something. You know how Papa always talks about his dog growing up?"

"Leroy," Oliver said. "A schnauzer."

"What a name," Orlando said.

"Leroy understood every word in the English language," Laney informed Orlando.

"He was pretty much a perfect angel, according to Papa's stories," Isa added. "A real-life Lassie or Benji."

"So you're thinking," Jessie said to Hyacinth, "that we can soften Mr. Huxley up by bringing New Dog back there, hoping she sparks memories of a beloved childhood dog that may or may not be named Buster, then create enough goodwill in him that he might consider letting us lease a space for Mama's bakery?"

Hyacinth looked back at Jessie. "Yes?"

"I like it," Jessie said, and her siblings and Orlando agreed.

They turned their attentions to New Dog and scrutinized her appearance. Laney, who had a hairbrush in her backpack, fluffed up New Dog's short fur to make her more presentable.

They were ready to face Mr. Huxley.

Thirty-Two

The Vanderbeekers, Orlando, and the dogs were almost at the front door of Herman's building when a water balloon fell to the ground in front of them and burst, getting nearly all of them wet. Laney and Hyacinth screamed. The dogs yelped.

"Hi!" Herman said, waving from the fourth-floor balcony. "Sorry to splash you!"

"What is *wrong* with you?" Oliver demanded.

"My building key is attached to the balloon," Herman called out. "I didn't want you to buzz in and tip off my dad."

Hyacinth looked on the ground, and there was the key, tied to a broken piece of balloon.

"You couldn't find a better way of getting us the

key?" Jessie yelled, shaking drops of water from the bottom of her pants.

"It was the only thing I had handy," Herman explained.

Jessie rolled her eyes, then used the key to enter the building. They synchronized their watches. Isa, Laney, Orlando, and the dogs stayed in the lobby, while Hyacinth, Oliver, and Jessie entered the shiny elevator and went up to the fourth floor.

Hyacinth rang the doorbell, and Herman, even though he was expecting them, did not answer. That was part of the plan.

Mr. Huxley opened the door, which was also part of the plan. Hyacinth could tell from his face that he was Not in the Mood to Talk, which was something the Vanderbeekers had accounted for.

"Herman is studying for state tests right now," Mr. Huxley told them.

"He's *studying* during spring break?" Oliver blurted out. Hyacinth nudged him in the ribs. "I mean, that's very . . . smart of him."

"It's an important academic year," Mr. Huxley said.

The Vanderbeekers nodded solemnly, as if they knew exactly what he meant. Which they didn't.

"I have a meeting to prepare for," Mr. Huxley said, and he started to shut the door.

Getting the door shut in their face was not part of the plan, and in an act of bravery that surprised even her, Hyacinth stuck out her foot to prevent it from closing.

"Can we ask you one thing?" Hyacinth said. Mr. Huxley looked as if he was going to say no, so Hyacinth hurried on. "Herman showed us some of your real estate listings, and there's one that we were really interested in."

Mr. Huxley sniffed. "I don't rent to kids."

Hyacinth knew that also translated into *I don't rent to Vanderbeekers,* but she didn't let that stop her. "It wouldn't be for us; it would be for my mom. She's a professional baker."

"She's amazing," Oliver said.

"If you tell us your favorite cookie, Mama can make them for you," Hyacinth said. "For free."

"Renting retail space is expensive, much more

expensive than cookies," Mr. Huxley told them, as if the Vanderbeekers did not know that.

"We were looking at the space on 143rd Street," Jessie said. "The really rundown one. Herman showed it to us. He said you were offering six months of free rent in return for renovations." She pulled the freshly printed business plan from her book bag. "Everything is in our business plan. Our goals and how we'll meet each one," Jessie told him. "The third page is particularly exciting, if I may say so myself." She handed him the document.

Mr. Huxley made no move to take it.

"I'm sure you'll find renting to us mutually beneficial," Oliver said. "That property would get cleaned up and renovated for free."

Mr. Huxley was not swayed. "That property is not a priority," he said. "It makes me no money."

"So you'll let us have it?" Laney asked.

"Absolutely not."

"But you wouldn't even have to do anything!" Oliver said. "We'd be doing *you* a favor."

Behind them, the elevator dinged. Isa came out with New Dog in tow.

"Hey, guys!" she said. "*Buster* and I thought we would check up on you."

Mr. Huxley stilled. "That dog's name is Buster?"

"Yep," said Isa. "She's the *sweetest*. We're fostering her."

"Uh-huh," Mr. Huxley said, and Hyacinth could tell from his reaction that the plan was going a little bit off the rails. She did her best to guide the train back on course.

"We're looking for a good home for her," Hyacinth said. "She's homeless."

"I had a dog named Buster once that looked just like that." Mr. Huxley pointed at New Dog, who whimpered and shrank under his glare.

"Oh, really?" Jessie said in the most nonchalant way she knew how. She tried to nudge New Dog closer to Mr. Huxley, but New Dog planted her feet and leaned back.

"Maybe *you* might want to adopt her," Isa ventured.

"She is super smart," Laney said. She looked at New Dog. "Sit," she commanded.

New Dog looked at her with wide eyes and wagged her tail tentatively. She did not sit.

"She's a work in progress," Jessie told Mr. Huxley.

Mr. Huxley looked back at the Vanderbeekers with bewilderment written all over his face. "Why would you ever think I would want a dog?"

"Um," Jessie said. "Because she reminds you of your childhood dog? Nostalgia, or something?"

Mr. Huxley waved a hand. "My dad made us give it away after a week. It ripped up the new carpet in the living room."

The Vanderbeekers cast one another worried glances. The glue that was holding the plan together was coming undone.

Unfortunately, Herman, unaware that the original plan had just gone awry, appeared in the doorway.

"Wow, what a cool dog!" Herman said.

Mr. Huxley turned to look at his son, and the Vanderbeekers all started waving wildly at him, trying to wordlessly convey, "Abort mission!" Herman was so focused on his lines that he didn't even notice.

"Oh wow!" he continued, dropping to the floor and petting New Dog with enthusiasm. "I wish we could get a dog. Dad, didn't you have a dog once?"

"Absolutely not," Mr. Huxley said. "Come on, I've got a meeting to prepare for."

"But—"

The door closed before Hyacinth could stick her foot in it again. The Vanderbeekers could hear Mr. Huxley's loud voice through the door. "I told you *not* to associate with that family!" Then they couldn't hear any more because Mr. Huxley and Herman moved further into their apartment. The Vanderbeekers were glad for that. Their voices were replaced by the building hallway's still, empty quiet.

As they got back in the elevator and left the building, their dream for securing Mama's bakery—a vision that had seemed so crystal clear just an hour earlier—popped like a bubble and floated off in the Harlem breeze.

* * *

After they left Mr. Huxley's, they headed home. When they got to 143rd Street, Laney detoured and beelined straight for the storefront. Her siblings and Orlando followed without a word.

Laney wanted to sweep the sidewalk of the storefront one more time. She had been so absolutely certain that this was the right place for Mama's bakery. Disappointment clogged her throat as the broom bristles whispered goodbye with every scrape of the sidewalk.

While Laney swept, the rest of the group sat on the stoop of the building next door and discussed their failed plan. A dog started barking from an open window, and as they looked up, a woman came into view—the same woman they had seen the day before with the dachshund. She waved when she saw the kids. They waved back, but without their typical enthusiasm. On the tree branch above the storefront, the same tuxedo cat watched them with round, unblinking eyes, her tail swishing in a figure-eight pattern. When the sidewalk was clean, Laney returned the broom to the restaurant next door, and the Vanderbeekers said goodbye to Orlando and headed home.

When they got to the brownstone, they looked through the living room window and saw Mama sitting at the dining room table, her huge accounting book opened before her. Her fingers were rubbing her temples, as if she had a headache.

Not wanting to disturb her, the kids headed up to Miss Josie and Mr. Jeet's apartment. When they knocked on the door, Miss Josie opened it to find five forlorn Vanderbeekers.

"Come in," Miss Josie said. "You look so cold! Come in and warm up." She opened the door wide, and everyone trooped in. Franz's nose immediately led him to the kitchen to look for fallen scraps, but New Dog went right into the bedroom to see Mr. Jeet.

Miss Josie looked at Laney. "I think Mr. Jeet wants to adopt New Dog."

Laney's eyes lit up. "Really?"

"Really," Miss Josie said. "But he's not the one who will have to walk her in all sorts of weather."

"I can walk her for you," Hyacinth offered. "I already walk Franz."

"We'll see," Miss Josie said, but she looked through the bedroom door at Mr. Jeet and New Dog and her eyes softened. "Now, what's got all of you so gloomy?"

Oliver flopped down on the couch and explained the whole situation. When he was done, Miss Josie went around and hugged all the Vanderbeekers. Then she said, "From where I'm standing, I see five kids who are growing up and wanting to do good in the world. And that fills me with hope."

And the brownstone creaked in agreement, wrapping the kids in warmth on that very cold, very bitter spring day.

* * *

That evening, Papa took Mama to dinner and a movie for her birthday, their annual tradition. The Vanderbeeker kids were left at home to feed the five kittens, one cat, two guinea pigs, two dogs, one rabbit, and seven chickens. When they were done, they collapsed on the couches in the living room, trying desperately to think of an amazing last-minute birthday gift for their mom.

Laney was the only one with an idea. She dragged out the big artist pad that Allegra had left behind and began writing enormous letters on the paper. Paganini hopped over the paper, scattering crayons, which led the kittens to bat the crayons until they rolled under the couch.

"What are you working on, Laney?" Isa said, looking over her sister's shoulder.

"Mama's present."

Isa leaned down and examined Laney's work. "Honey, you know we didn't get the store, right?"

Laney concentrated on writing the most perfect "C" she could. "I know that."

"Then what is this for?"

"Mama's birthday present," Laney repeated. "We can't give up. Mr. Beiderman and Herman *and* Miss Josie all said that."

Isa sighed. "We tried everything. It's impossible."

"It's not," Laney said. "It's only impossible if we give up."

Isa stared at her youngest sister for a long moment. Then she took a deep breath and said, "Can I help?"

Laney looked up. "Only if you can make it super-duper good."

"I know just the right person to ask." Isa picked up her phone and texted Allegra. "Help needed, pronto," she typed.

"Oliver," Isa called. "You have some leftover boards from the treehouse, right?"

Oliver nodded.

"Can you get them? We've got a project to do tonight."

APRIL

MONDAY	TUESDAY	WEDNESDAY
1	2 Find homes for kittens! S·	3 Find homes for kittens and guinea pigs! P·R·I·N·G

SATURDAY, APRIL 6

Thirty-Three

The next morning, the Vanderbeeker kids woke up at five o'clock, even though waking up that early on a weekend was a special type of torture.

Mama always said that breakfast was her favorite meal of the day, and the Vanderbeekers had decided the night before that she needed a Surprise Birthday Breakfast Shindig. When Isa's alarm went off, she hopped out of bed and dragged her four sleepy siblings out of their beds. They made sure the white-noise machine was on in their parents' room (it was), fed the eighteen animals, then got to work in the kitchen.

Hyacinth was the originator of the breakfast-party idea, and she had a very specific vision. She gave her siblings the menu: an omelet bar with lots of vegetable and cheese options, granola with fruit and nut topping choices, breakfast cookies, and her favorite idea of all: a smoothie bar with a variety of frozen fruit, yogurt, and juice. Guests were instructed to arrive at eight twenty on the dot, and there was a lot to do before they came.

Oliver, who had impressive chopping skills, got to work cutting up bell peppers, onions, and tomatoes for the omelets. Jessie was in charge of the smoothie station, Isa prepared the granola, and Hyacinth assigned herself to the cookies. Laney set up the cereal bar, utensils, and napkins.

Laney posted herself by the door at eight twenty, and to her amazement, people were right on time, bearing gifts of the most bizarre kitchen tools they could find (also part of the Surprise Birthday Breakfast Shindig instructions). By eight thirty, the living room was filled with their favorite people, everyone in their pajamas: Auntie Harrigan and Uncle Arthur and Mr. Beiderman, Mr. Jones the postman and Herman Huxley, Mr. Smiley and Angie, Jimmy L and his mom, Allegra, Benjamin and his parents, and even quiet Mr.

Ritchie, who operated the flower and Christmas tree stand across the river. Orlando and Miss Josie had helped Mr. Jeet down the stairs, and they settled him into his wheelchair by the kitchen.

Everyone crouched behind couches and hid in corners. A few minutes later, when Mama's bedroom door opened and they saw her appear at the top of the stairs, everyone popped out from their respective hiding places and yelled, "Happy birthday!"

Mama froze. Her hands went first to her mouth, then to her hair. She turned around and disappeared from sight. "I love you all!" she called. "But I need to brush my teeth and hair first!"

The brownstone rocked with laughter, and soon the Vanderbeeker home was filled with the voices of friends and the aroma of onions frying and omelets cooking. Mama came downstairs, her teeth clean and her hair brushed. She exclaimed over everyone, complimented Mr. Beiderman's polka-dotted pajamas ("Your kids said I had to wear these," Mr. B grumbled), gave out lots of hugs, and laughed at the elaborate breakfast bar.

"A surprise pajama breakfast birthday party?" Mama beamed at her kids. "I cannot imagine a more perfect celebration!"

Mama visited all the food bars and loaded up her plate with an omelet and a breakfast cookie. She sampled Laney's cereal recommendations and requested a mango lassi at the smoothie station. Once she was done eating, the Vanderbeeker kids urged her to open presents from the rest of the guests. Some were useful (the whisk wiper), some funny (dachshund dog corn holders), and others ridiculous (oven mitts made to look like enormous bear paws). People chatted and laughed and Papa put music on, and for a moment everyone forgot that Mama's baking business was officially closed.

And that was when the phone rang.

❁ ❁ ❁

Oliver was closest. He picked up the phone. "Hello, Vanderbeeker residence."

A woman's voice came through the line. "Hello? Is there a Ms. Vanderbeeker there?"

"She's at her Surprise Birthday Breakfast Shindig

right now," Oliver yelled over the party noise. "Can she call you back later?"

"Oh, I do love birthdays," the woman said. "Can she spare a quick minute?"

"Who's calling?" Oliver asked.

"This is Shirley Adelaide Chester, at your service."

"O-kay." Oliver had never heard of a Shirley Addie Whatever, but he put down the phone and interrupted Mama's conversation with Mr. Jones. "Some lady named Shirley is on the phone for you, and she doesn't sound like a telemarketer."

Mama apologized to Mr. Jones and followed Oliver to the phone. Oliver could only hear Mama's side of the conversation, and it sounded pretty bizarre.

"Thank you . . . Really? . . . No, they never mentioned anything . . . Well, I don't know . . . I do have a job interview this Monday, actually . . . Is that right? . . . I guess we should head over? . . . All right, I'll ask them . . . See you soon, Mrs. Chester."

Mama hung up the phone and looked at Oliver, then at his sisters, who all sensed that something was up and had gathered around with Papa.

"That was Shirley Adelaide Chester," Mama said. "She wants me to meet her on 143rd Street."

"On 143rd Street?" every single one of the Vanderbeeker kids said at the same time.

"I'm assuming you know who Shirley Adelaide Chester is?" Mama inquired, her eyebrow raised at her kids' reactions.

The kids looked at one another in bewilderment.

"Honestly, Mama," Isa said. "We have no idea who she is . . . but we *have* been spending some time on 143rd Street."

"Why?" Mama asked.

Oliver swallowed. "It would make the most sense to show it to you." His siblings nodded in agreement.

Papa squinted at his kids. "This isn't dangerous, is it?"

They shook their heads.

"Illegal? Expensive? Something that will make us ground you until you're senior citizens?"

Again they shook their heads.

Mama glanced at Papa, and he nodded.

"Let's go," Mama said.

Oliver grabbed the secret wrapped project they had

worked on the night before. Hyacinth safely stored the kittens in their crate home, Laney shoved her arms into her coat sleeves before grabbing Mama's hand, Jessie and Isa leashed up Franz and New Dog, and off they all went to 143rd Street. The birthday party guests, intrigued by this last-minute development, followed.

"And now we're going outside in our pajamas," Mr. Beiderman complained.

"It's never a dull day with the Vanderbeekers," Uncle Arthur commented.

The morning air was crisp, the kind of air that felt good against your face and inside your lungs. Puffy clouds that looked as if they had come right off the ceilings of the New York Public Library's main branch dotted the sky and reflected against the brownstone windows.

The entire breakfast party made its way across 141st Street, up Malcolm X Boulevard, and eastward on 143rd Street. It was a bizarre yet joyful procession of dogs, kids, and adults of all ages marching along in their pajamas. Papa pushed Mr. Jeet in his wheelchair, and New Dog insisted on trotting right next to them.

In addition to her flannel pajamas, Mama was wearing the birthday hat Hyacinth had made, a felt creation festooned with feathers and flowers.

When they arrived, 143rd Street was positively sleepy. Only one woman—with a dachshund in a sweater with a hot dog on it—was to be seen on the sidewalk, the same woman and dog they had seen yesterday from the window and on their first trip to the storefront. She was standing in front of the Not-to-Be Bakery, her hair flipping gently in the breeze. In her hand was one of their kitten posters.

Franz and New Dog barked their greetings to the dachshund, and the Vanderbeekers kneeled down to pat the adorable low-rider on the head.

"Hi again," Laney said to the woman. She pointed at the kitten poster. "Did you change your mind about adopting a kitten?"

"No," the woman said back, "but this poster did help me find you. I'm Shirley Adelaide Chester," she said. Then she turned to Mama. "And I wanted to let you know that if you want this place, you can have it."

"That's so . . . generous of you," Mama said, then looked at the kids. "Am I missing something?"

"You're giving this to us?" Laney asked, her eyes as round as cherries.

"But how? I thought it belonged to Mr. Huxley," Isa said, confusion written in the creases of her forehead.

"It certainly does *not* belong to Mr. Huxley," Shirley Adelaide Chester said, frowning. "I live on the third floor, and the owner of the building has been trying to get someone to take over this retail lease for ages. But the last tenant left it in such a wreck, and the building owner never had money to renovate. It's been sitting here like an eyesore, and then I overheard you kids talking about how you want to make it into a bakery for your mom. I watched you sweep and clean the front. Well, you bet I called the building owner right away and let him know."

Mama froze. "A bakery?"

"But Mr. Huxley said he would never let us lease this place in a million years," Oliver said.

"Well, good thing he doesn't own the building," Ms. Chester said. "We fired him."

"Fired him?" Hyacinth asked. "You can do that?" She glanced at Herman. He shrugged, completely unconcerned that his dad had been fired.

"We sure can," Ms. Chester said. "There's more than one real estate broker in Harlem, and after a few calls, we hired a new agent, who will represent our interests. And here we are! If you think you can renovate it, it's yours."

Hyacinth turned to Herman. "I'm sorry we made your dad lose the space."

"It's fine. He thinks it's a dump." Herman looked at Ms. Chester. "No offense."

"Uncle Arthur can renovate it!" Laney said.

"I can?" Uncle Arthur said, still trying to keep up with what was going on.

"I can help on the weekends," Mr. Smiley offered.

"Me too," Papa said. "Ooh, can I use your power tools?" he asked Uncle Arthur.

Mama raised her arms in the air. "Wait. Just . . . wait. This is moving too fast. I can't do something like this. And I can't ask all of you to give up your time to make it happen." One trembling hand covered her mouth.

"But Mama," Isa said, "this *has* been the plan all along, hasn't it?"

Oliver picked up the project they had all worked on

the night before and propped it up in front of Mama. Her hands still shaking, she pulled the paper off the front. When she saw the big café sign, designed by Allegra and painted by her children, she really did cry.

"Mama," Isa said, "you should use the Fiver Account to renovate this space."

Mama shook her head. "But that's our travel money. We've been saving for years."

"And we're going to save again," Jessie said. Then each of the Vanderbeeker kids handed her a birthday card with a picture of what they thought her dream vacation destination was. The choices included Paris, Bangkok, Monterey Bay, Prince Edward Island, and Disney World. Inside each card was a five-dollar bill. This, of course, only made Mama cry more.

It took a moment for her to control herself, but when she could talk again, she waved her hands in front of her face and said, "Happy tears. These are happy tears."

And the Vanderbeeker kids surrounded Mama and Papa, and surrounding *them* were Auntie Harrigan and Uncle Arthur and Mr. Jeet and Miss Josie, and surrounding *them* was their hodgepodge of a community, connected not by blood but by an abundance of love.

The next day, the Vanderbeeker kids would all remember different things from that moment. Isa would remember having a great sense of peace about her audition the day before, a peace she had not remembered feeling for months. Jessie would remember noticing that she was now taller than her mom, a discovery that surprised and stunned her. Oliver had been squeezed in on all sides, and even though he did not enjoy having the air sucked out of his lungs, he would remember feeling like the luckiest kid in the world. Hyacinth would remember Franz wriggling around and howling, the feel of his paws stepping on her sneakers and making her heart warm and content. And Laney . . . Laney would remember thinking that with all this good news, her parents were certain to let her adopt Tuxedo the kitten and maybe even the guinea pigs, whom she had already secretly named Anne and Diana.

In the end, the Vanderbeeker kids did all agree on one thing: as they were smooshed in the middle of the twenty-three-person hug, standing in front of what would soon become Mama's bakery, they could all smell the barest hint of sea salt caramel chocolate cookies on the breeze.

Epilogue

Five months later

PERCH MAGAZINE

Where to Find the Best Cookies in New York City? Try Harlem's New Cat Café

By Nina Walker

If you were to take a walk along 143rd Street in Harlem, you might notice a charming bakery painted white and trimmed in pink. Look up, and most likely a tuxedo cat peering at you with curiosity, perched on a branch growing out of the sidewalk. A large picture window graces the front of the bakery, and flowers tumble in a flurry of color from the planters on either side of the door. Take a closer look through the window, and you might see a cat snoozing in a hammock or basking in the afternoon sun, and a pair of kittens scrambling up the maze built into one wall. Welcome to the Treehouse Bakery and Cat Café, Harlem's newest must-see cookie spot.

The first cat café opened in Taiwan in 1998, but the trend truly took off in Japan. In Japanese cities, where many apartment buildings restrict pet ownership, the cat café provided a perfect opportunity for those wanting some cat companionship. The trend traveled to America, where multiple cat cafés have achieved great success. The Treehouse Bakery and Cat Café is the newest, opened by Harlem resident Maia Vanderbeeker this month.

"I love coming here after work," said Shirley Adelaide Chester, a neighbor and frequent customer, as she enjoyed a "Cat-puccino" and cuddled a ten-week-old tabby named Jubilee. "Petting these cats is like getting a dose of sunshine in your body."

The Treehouse Bakery and Cat Café has twelve cats living there at any given time. They are all rescues and up for adoption, and a bulletin board holds photos and detailed descriptions of the cats. All potential adopters must fill out an application and have a home visit before taking ownership of their new furry friends.

You can find Maia in the kitchen six days a week. There she bakes around one thousand cookies every day for the shop and for special events. The menu changes with the seasons (pumpkin butterscotch cookies and maple brown sugar cookies are the current specials), but two neighborhood favorites are available every day: chocolate sea salt caramel cookies and double chocolate pecan cookies. Get there in the morning—cookies often sell out by early afternoon—and plan to return again and again.

The Treehouse Bakery and Cat Café
Open Tuesday through Sunday, 8 a.m.–6 p.m.
125 West 143rd Street, New York, NY 10030

Acknowledgments

As always, it has been an honor to work with Ann Rider, my brilliant editor at HMH Books for Young Readers. I am grateful for her insight, intuition, and, most of all, her kindness. Tara Shanahan is the best publicist an author could wish for, and I feel so incredibly lucky to have her working on my books. Many thanks to Celeste Knudsen and Lisa Vega for the beautiful book design, to Katya Longhi for the gorgeous book cover, and to Jennifer Thermes for the lovely Harlem map endpapers. I absolutely adore Lisa DiSarro and Amanda Acevedo, HMH's amazing school and library marketing team; I appreciate all of their hard work putting the Vanderbeekers into the hands of teachers and librarians. A huge hug to Tara

Sonin, Alia Almeida, and Emma Gordon for supporting me and celebrating each milestone, and to all the HMH sales reps who travel miles and miles to share books with booksellers. I'm incredibly grateful to Cat Onder, John Sellers, Mary Magrisso, Candace Finn, Elizabeth Agyemang, and Mary Wilcox for all that they do (they each do A LOT!). Special thanks to Colleen Fellingham, Alix Redmond, and Erika West for their watchful copyeditor eyes.

I adore my Curtis Brown family who have cheered me on and advocated on my behalf these past few years. In particular, my agent Ginger Clark deserves a lifetime of wombat happiness. Thank you, Holly Frederick, for championing the Vanderbeekers and for having big dreams for me, and Tess Callero, for all of your social media awesomeness.

Librarians, teachers, booksellers, readers—thank you for your enthusiasm for the Vanderbeekers and for letting them into your hearts. You are the best!

I am so grateful for Amy Poehler, Kim Lessinger, and the Paper Kite team for loving the Vanderbeekers and these stories!

The Kid Lit community is an incredible one, and

there are so many who have encouraged me and cheered me on—too many to list! A special shout-out to my critique partners, Laura Shovan, Casey Lyall, Timanda Wertz, Margaret Dilloway, Leah Henderson, Ki-Wing Merlin, and Lauren Hart, who read early drafts of this book and gave invaluable feedback.

Huge hugs to Lauren Hart, Emily Rabin, Katie Graves-Abe, Harrigan Bowman, Desiree Welsing, Janice Nimura, the Glaser family, and the Dickinson family for being wonderful, amazing people. In addition, lots of love to the communities that have inspired and encouraged me, including the Town School, the Town School Book Club, Book Riot, Read-Aloud Revival, the New York Society Library, the New York Public Library, the Book Cellar, All Angels' Church, and my Harlem neighbors.

Lastly, I have the opportunity to pursue my writing dream because of the loving support of the three most important people in my life: Dan, Kaela, and Lina. I love them to the moon and back.

Look for more

VANDERBEEKERS

adventures in 2020!

The Vanderbeekers Lost and Found

When autumn arrives on 141st Street, the Vanderbeekers are busy helping Mr. Beiderman get ready for the New York City Marathon, planning their neighborhood's Halloween 5K Fun Run, and making sure the mysterious person sleeping in the community garden gets enough to eat. But when they discover the true identity of the person making their home in the shed of the community garden, their world turns upside down as they learn what it means to care for and love someone in an impossible situation.

In this fourth book in the Vanderbeekers series, return to 141st Street and experience another season with Isa, Jessie, Oliver, Hyacinth, and Laney as they attempt to make their neighborhood a better place, one hilarious, impossible plan at a time.

HARLEM
THE BROWNSTONE ON 141st STREET
Jimmy L's Apartment
Garden
Church
Mr. Smiley & Angie's Building
Allegra's Apartment
Harlem Coffee
Library
A to Z Deli
Castleman's Bakery
Hilba's Hardware Store
City College
St. Nicholas Park
Orlando's Place
Animal Care Center
AMSTERDAM AVENUE
CONVENT AVENUE
HAMILTON TERRACE
EDGECOMBE AVENUE
ST. NICHOLAS AVE.
FREDERICK DOUGLASS BLVD.
ADAM CLAYTON POWELL JR. BLVD.
MALCOLM X BLVD
141st Street
138th Street
137th Street
136th Street
135th Street
134th Street
133rd Street
132nd Street
131st Street
130th Street
129th Street
128th Street
127th Street
126th Street
125th Street
124th Street
123rd Street
122nd Street
121st Street